Give Me Another Chance, COWBOY

CAVANAGH COWBOYS ROMANCE - 2

VALERIE COMER

Greenwords Media

Valerie Comer Bibliography

Urban Farm Fresh Romance

0. Promise of Peppermint (ebook only)
1. Secrets of Sunbeams
2. Butterflies on Breezes
3. Memories of Mist
4. Wishes on Wildflowers
5. Flavors of Forever
6. Raindrops on Radishes
7. Dancing at Daybreak
8. Glimpses of Gossamer
9. Lavished with Lavender
10. Cadence of Cranberries
11. Joys of Juniper

Christmas in Montana Romance

1. More Than a Tiara
2. Other Than a Halo
3. Better Than a Crown

Farm Fresh Romance

1. Raspberries and Vinegar
2. Wild Mint Tea
3. Sweetened with Honey
4. Dandelions for Dinner
5. Plum Upside Down
6. Berry on Top

Cavanagh Cowboys Romance
(Montana Ranches Christian Romance)

1. Marry Me for Real, Cowboy'
2. Give Me Another Chance, Cowboy
3. Let Me Off Easy, Cowboy

Saddle Springs Romance
(Montana Ranches Christian Romance)

1. The Cowboy's Christmas Reunion
2. The Cowboy's Mixed-Up Matchmaker
3. The Cowboy's Romantic Dreamer
4. The Cowboy's Convenient Marriage
5. The Cowboy's Belated Discovery
6. The Cowboy's Reluctant Bride

Garden Grown Romance
(Arcadia Valley Romance)

1. Sown in Love (ebook only)
2. Sprouts of Love
3. Rooted in Love
4. Harvest of Love

Riverbend Romance Novellas

1. Secretly Yours
2. Pinky Promise
3. Sweet Serenade
4. Team Bride
5. Merry Kisses

valeriecomer.com/books

CHAPTER ONE

Y ou're late." Travis Cavanagh planted his cowboy boots in the dust beside the corral and parked his fists on his hips. "Twenty minutes."

"Because this is somehow the end of the world as we know it?" Dakota Erickson swung out of her compact car. "Because you've never once been late bringing Toby back to town on a Sunday afternoon?"

Travis reached for the backdoor handle as much to block the sight of Dakota's long legs as to release his son from the confines of his car seat. "Hi, cowpoke."

"Daddy!" Toby bounced out of the car and launched himself at Travis.

His kid made putting up with Dakota worth it. Dakota, who still had the power to slice Travis down to size with a single sneer. Yeah, he asked for it. Could he plead self-defense? Because he couldn't let her see how she still affected him. She didn't need the ammunition. Travis hoisted Toby to the corral rail beside him before daring to glance at Dakota again.

She was gorgeous. Always had been, even as a teen, but managing a western wear shop had finally enabled her to dress the part. She'd grown into her beauty. He'd rather not look, but it was hard to resist.

That was behind him. The only thing linking them together now was Toby, who was a bittersweet reminder of all that had been and all that could have been if Travis hadn't been such a hothead. It didn't matter that he'd give anything to replay those days and come up with a different outcome.

Dakota was done with him, which meant he was done with her.

Except for their four-year-old.

"Are you finished ogling me?"

He blinked Dakota into focus. If nothing else snapped him back to reality, it was the cool disdain on her face as she gathered her long dark hair in one hand and tossed it over her shoulder.

She's just trying to rattle you, dude.

But Travis could match the chill. He raised his eyebrows, gave her a slow once-over from her pretty face, down her snap-front shirt with its fringed yoke, slim-fitting jeans, and red cowboy boots, then back up. "Done now. Got a problem with that?"

"Here's the rest of the view." She spun on one heel, keeping her gaze fixed on his.

"Very nice. You might want to take the tags off that shirt, though."

She started to reach for her collar then glared at him. "I already did."

"Made you check." And now he felt like he had the

upper hand. Juvenile. He knew it, but that had never kept him from seeking high ground. High *moral* ground, however, he'd ditched a long time ago, as evidenced by the child they shared.

Toby. Travis reached for his little sidekick on the log rail, but his hand came up empty. He pivoted, panic beginning to claw at his throat, only to hear his son's high toddler voice. "I feeds Clover."

Travis's thirteen-year-old half-sister answered. "Sure. Here's an apple slice for your pony."

"One of these times you're going to lose him completely if you don't pay closer attention." Dakota's glare turned full North Pole cold. "Maybe we should revisit our schedule."

"He's fine with Emma." And this, right here, was why Travis did his best to be out fencing or riding or cutting hay or anything at all on a Friday afternoon. Not because he didn't want to spend every single second he could with his son, but because Dakota made him second-guess absolutely every decision he made, starting with which boot to put on first in the morning.

Dakota glanced toward the open stable door. "I'll just give him a kiss and be on my way."

"Do you have to drag it out? He's fine. You can hear it for yourself."

Right on cue, Toby giggled, and Emma laughed with him.

"Just because you're a cold, uncaring parent doesn't mean I have to be."

What on earth? "What makes you think I don't care? He's my kid. Of course, I care."

"Right." She skirted around him and entered the stable.

"Hi, Emma. Good thing you were here. Bye, buddy. See you Sunday. Be a good boy for Emma and Daddy."

"I's always good." The sound of his smacking kiss nearly wiped the scowl from Travis's face.

Might have succeeded if Dakota hadn't managed additional digs at his parenting in that brief exchange, as though his little sister was more responsible than he was.

"Bye, Trav. Try not to be late dropping him off on Sunday, okay? I have plans for the evening, and I'd rather not wait around." She slid into her car.

His blood pressure spiked again. "I'll be just as considerate of you as you are of me."

Dakota's window rolled down a couple of inches. "How about being a grownup here? Some of us don't live with Daddy anymore or take our orders from him every morning. Some of us had to embrace becoming an adult for, you know, assorted reasons." She arched her brows with a pointed look toward the stable. "See you Sunday."

She cranked her engine, whipped the little clunker into reverse, and peeled around until she faced the long ranch driveway. Then she scattered gravel and dust as she sped away.

Which was the perfect time for his father to storm out of the tack room, scowling. Travis groaned as Declan turned toward him.

"Would you remind her how far dust flies on this ranch? A little respect goes a long way."

"It's not like she listens to anything I say." Even to himself, Travis's voice sounded petulant. If his dad had overheard the entire exchange, Travis was hooped anyway.

"Wear the pants in your family."

Oh, because Dad was such a great example of that? Declan had driven Travis's mother to file for divorce and shunted his current wife into a suite of rooms in the big ranch house's walk-out basement. Not that Kathryn wasn't allowed off the ranch, of course, but it was clear to their six his-and-hers sons and their two shared daughters that Declan and Kathryn had anything but a cooperative marriage. Dad was a fine one to be spouting relationship advice.

Reminding him of that had never gone over well.

Travis strode into the stable to find his son. He needed to block out all that negative stuff and spoil the kid as much as he could in forty-eight hours.

Declan might not be a doting grandfather, but at least he allowed Travis to have Toby at the ranch every weekend without a hassle.

Travis scooped Toby away from Emma. "Thanks for watching him a minute. Hey, cowpoke, ready for a ride with Daddy?"

"On Clover? Yes!"

Getting Toby his own pony for his fourth birthday had been a brilliant idea. "Let's go then."

DAKOTA WAS STILL FUMING when she pulled in her drive and spotted her neighbor out watering the flower bed beside her front door.

"Hey, Dakota!"

"Hi, Sage." Since Sage's roommate had married and moved out a month ago, the woman had been a lot needier than before. Today, though, Dakota wasn't into it. Movie night with a bunch of romantic chick-flicks held no appeal.

"Toby's off to the ranch?"

Just like every weekend, but Sage knew that. Dakota nodded.

"Want to do something?"

"Sorry, not tonight. I… need to get some orders placed at the store."

"Aw, you never take time off."

Which was pretty much true. And Sage needed something to occupy herself with. "You should sign up for the Pot of Gold Treasure Hunt this summer. Creekside Fellowship is hosting that again, right?"

"I wish you'd come to church with me."

Not a chance. Attending Creekside would mean watching Travis and his family interact with Toby, and Dakota couldn't handle it. "I'm happy at Grace."

"But there are hardly any young singles there."

Dakota shrugged. "I don't mind. I'm not looking for anyone." Except for Travis to change into a decent man, which wouldn't happen for a few more decades, if ever. "Seriously, though, why not join the geocaching hunt? It sounds like fun and a great way to make new friends."

"I'll do it if you do."

"Sorry. You've got way more free time than I do. I don't think Toby would appreciate being dragged up and down hiking trails every night." And she definitely wasn't giving Travis an opening for more time with their son.

On the flip side, it was always entertaining when he assumed she was dating someone else. She did it once in a while just to check if Travis still had a beating heart. Turns out he did jealous really well. So well she usually let the rumors float while she stayed in the duplex and ate popcorn. If he could dig at her, she could dig back.

"There's a gymkhana this weekend out at the fairgrounds. Travis ever put him in something like that?"

Now that shot Dakota straight back to her teens. She feigned nonchalance. "He's never mentioned the idea to me. Besides, Toby's just turned four." Dakota twirled her car keys and glanced toward her front door. "He's really too young."

Travis wouldn't want to start their son down the path to rodeo, would he? Sure, he and Dakota had thrived in that environment when they were kids. Informal races, whittling their riding and roping skills, with some of them hoping for the big time. Like Travis's stepbrother, Adam, who'd done well for himself in pro rodeo after getting started in local events.

No way did Dakota want that life for her baby. Adam had made good money, but by risking his neck every time he rode? Her mama heart couldn't handle the thought.

Better he turned out like Adam than like Dakota's own brother, though.

Sage looped the hose around its bib. "You and Travis ever going to patch things up?"

"Who said I wanted to?"

"You're always a little grumpy when you get back on Friday afternoons. I thought it might have something to do with unrequited love."

Dakota managed a laugh. "Oh, you're such a dreamer. Fix things with Caleb Grant if you want a project." Travis may have been homeschooled out at Rockstead Ranch, but

Dakota had attended the public high school just a couple of years behind Sage and Caleb. She remembered the item they'd been then and how they avoided each other like the plague now, although they did attend the same church. Sage was a braver soul than Dakota.

"Nothing to fix." Sage waved an airy hand. "We've been over each other forever."

"Uh huh. Tell yourself what you need to hear." Dakota edged toward her front door. "Talk to you later." Then she completed her getaway, sighing with relief as she leaned against the closed door from inside.

She should probably look for a new rental if she didn't want to see her neighbor, but Sage was nearly the only friend she had. And wasn't that sort of upheaval bad for kids? Toby shifted between his parents every weekend as it was. He had his own western-style bedroom and a few sets of clothes in his dad's cabin, and a Toy-Story-themed bedroom at home. Not much went back and forth with him. Except for...

Dakota's gaze landed down the hallway where a plush Woody lay abandoned in the doorway to her son's room. Hadn't she stuffed that in Toby's pack? She was sure she had, but had she zipped it?

She groaned. This was not going to be pretty. On the other hand, Travis could handle it. Right? Except he wouldn't discover the missing toy until he was tucking a sleepy little boy in bed, and then — boom — the screaming fits would start. Then he'd phone her and beg her to drive back up to Rockstead, and she'd be frustrated, and... she already was.

If it were just Travis, she'd let him deal with it. But it

was her young son who'd take hours to sob himself to sleep, and she couldn't live with herself, knowing how traumatized he'd be. If a mama could fix things before they happened and keep the peace, she needed to do that.

Dakota tugged her phone out of her hip pocket and tapped Travis's number. It rang the requisite three times and went to voicemail. Figured. Rockstead Ranch didn't have cell coverage except near the main house and stables, which meant Travis was terrible about keeping his phone on him. And even worse about picking up when it was her, especially on the weekend.

She could leave him a message and then hang around and wait for his reply, or she could do the adult thing and drive the stuffed doll up to Rockstead right now. Then it would be off her mind, and no one would be traumatized, except possibly Travis when she showed up a second time today.

That's what a good mom would do, and she was a good mom.

And she'd reward herself for going the extra mile — sixty extra miles, actually, if she counted both directions — by getting takeout from the Golden Grill on her way back into town.

She grabbed the plush toy and glanced around Toby's room to make sure there was nothing else he needed but, of course, there wasn't.

He had everything else he needed at his dad's… except his mama.

CHAPTER TWO

Daddy, gots a free? Go fish!"

Travis glanced at the clock. The airhorn was going to sound for dinner any time. He could stand a few more minutes of this boring kiddie game for his son's sake.

A sharp rat-a-tat-tat sounded on his door, and he frowned. Definitely didn't sound like one of his siblings.

"Who that, Daddy?"

On the other hand, it was a distraction from the game, and that could only be good. He whisked the door open and blinked, stepping backward. "Dakota?" A quick glance toward the parking area didn't reveal her car. Which didn't change the fact that she was on his doorstep for the first time in... ages.

She extended their son's favorite stuffed toy. "You might need this."

"Mama!" Toby scrambled off the chair and flung himself at Dakota's legs. "Woody!"

"Hey, buddy." She swung him to her hip as Toby

squished his toy under his arm. He plastered Dakota's cheek with kisses.

Man, she looked good — natural — holding Travis's kid. Whatever their issues, and they had plenty, she was a good mother.

"We mustn't have zipped up your backpack tight, and Woody was sad you'd gone on an adventure without him. We couldn't let that happen, could we?"

"No. Woody need 'ventures, too."

"He does. I didn't want to hear him cry because he was lonely for you."

Personifying the toy was ridiculous. "Uh, thanks. I'd have met you halfway if I'd known."

"I would have appreciated it, but you didn't answer your phone."

He hadn't? It was in his jacket pocket, which was where? In the stable. Oh.

Dakota closed her eyes for a few seconds then lowered Toby to the floor. She gave a sigh and straightened her spine. "So, if you had, I wouldn't have run out of gas on the ranch road."

He bellowed a laugh but chopped it off right quick when he saw her expression shuttering. "You're serious." The perfect person who did everything by the book hadn't checked her fuel gauge? He never thought he'd see the day.

The airhorn announcing dinner blasted down the row of cabins where most of the Cavanagh brothers lived. Blake came out of his nearby cabin and did a doubletake seeing Dakota on Travis's step. "Hi, uh, you here for supper?"

Great. Tardiness at mealtime wasn't allowed. By the

time he'd filled a jerry can with fuel, taken the four-wheeler who knew how far down the drive to get Dakota on her way, and come back to the house, the meal would be more than half over, and Declan would run him through the wringer. Better to ask Cook to set an extra plate. There was always enough.

He turned to Dakota. "Good idea. I'll get you back on the road after we eat."

"I'm not having dinner anywhere near your family, thank you very much. I'll wait right here." She plopped down on the cabin steps.

Just what he needed.

Adam and his bride came out of their cabin a couple of doors down, hand in hand. Riley's face brightened when she caught sight of Dakota. "Hey! I haven't seen you in a while."

Travis and his stepbrother might hate each other's guts, but somehow the women had become solid friends, right down to Riley asking Dakota to be in their wedding party. That'd stung plenty, not that Travis had wanted the same invitation from Adam. Not a hope.

Adam jerked his chin in Dakota's direction. "What's going on?"

"She ran out of gas."

"I'll give you a hand."

Travis didn't *need* a hand. On the flip side, Adam didn't give a rip if Declan shredded him for being late. He'd take the lion's share of the blame with Declan then wheedle Cook out of food for them both. Win, win.

Travis nodded. "Okay."

Riley looped her arm through Dakota's. "And you can

keep me company through dinner. Come on, scamp!" She reached for Toby's hand.

Dakota shot Travis a panicked look, but he only smiled and extended his palm for her keys. What he wouldn't give to see her face up to his dad. That'd be fun for everyone.

"How far down?" he called after them.

"Couple of miles."

No wonder she was cranky. Crankier than usual, that is. That was the steep part of the drive, and those sexy boots she wore were made for riding, not hiking. Maybe they were more for catching some guy's attention. Not him, of course. Those days between them were long gone.

"I'll bring the ATV around if you want to fill a fuel can."

"Sure." Why was Adam being so nice to him? He'd mellowed out a ton since quitting the rodeo and coming home six months ago with his fake fiancée in tow. Turned out the laugh was on him, since the pair were now married. Wasn't that just like Adam? The guy was so happy-go-lucky that the waters of the Red Sea would part just for him.

Unlike Travis. Nothing ever went his way.

Including dinner.

He squeezed the nozzle at the base of the elevated gas tank and filled the fuel can while Adam rumbled over on the all-terrain vehicle. Travis strapped the can down and mounted behind his stepbrother.

By the time they roared past the house, everyone appeared to have gone inside. Dakota was in good hands with Riley. If anyone could stand up to Declan, it was her. Must be nice not to have all the history with the tyrannical rancher like Declan's three sons and three stepsons did.

Adam slid around a corner and swerved around Dakota's car. "Whoa!" he shouted as he throttled down. "Wasn't expecting it right there."

Travis unstrapped the can and began pouring its contents into the tank.

"What was she doing at Rockstead, anyway? Didn't she drop Toby off an hour or two ago?"

"Yeah. She forgot Toby's favorite toy. I should probably pick up a duplicate so we don't have to worry about things like that in the future."

"It won't have the same threadbare marks."

Travis shrugged as he tipped the fuel can away from the car and screwed down the cap. "Close enough."

"I think you know better."

Like he needed his least favorite stepbrother to point that out. "Leave it."

"And while you're thinking that through—"

"I'm not."

"—you might consider talking things out with Dakota."

Travis hoisted the jerry can to the four-wheeler's cargo area and strapped it back down. "Anything else?" Couldn't quite manage to tamp out all the annoyance in his voice. Oops. Color him sorry.

"It'd sure be nice for Toby to have his parents on the same page."

"Because nothing says love like having your parents fight every single day until one of them walks out." Travis gave Adam a hard stare. "You didn't get to experience that. You got the other card, the my-dad-died card. And I am sure that was rough." He held up both hands.

Adam opened his mouth and closed it again.

"But I can tell you, nothing beats your parents yelling at each other for at least a decade before your mom walks out and leaves behind three little kids without even a backward glance. You know what that told me? It told me I'm not worth sticking around for. My mother didn't. Dakota didn't. And the way things are right now, Toby has two parents. There's no way I'm rocking that boat, because a kid needs a mother *and* a father. Got it?"

"Me'n Riley are praying for you, dude."

"Thanks." Travis clipped the word. He meant it. Nothing but prayer could fix anything. But this mess with Dakota? Seemed too big for even God.

"I DON'T WANT to go in there." Dakota grasped Riley's arm. "This family terrifies me."

"No one will bite. I won't let them."

"C'mon, Mama!" Toby pulled her hand. "Cook makes my fav'rite."

It wasn't the food she was worried about. It was Declan's hard stare and Travis's brothers' curiosity.

"You can do it." Riley gave her a smile and pushed open the door. The cowboys milling in the foyer silenced immediately, looking between them.

"I told them she was here," said Blake. "Dad, too."

"Thanks." Didn't make it much less awkward.

"Ladies first." Travis's stepbrother Nathaniel gestured them forward. "And kids." He tweaked Toby's nose.

"Hi, Unca Nat."

Dakota still couldn't believe Travis allowed his stepbrothers to be called uncles by Toby. She shook her head as she followed Riley into the dining room.

Travis's stepmother, Kathryn, rose from her place at the foot. "Welcome, Dakota. Hello, little man."

Toby ran over and hugged Kathryn's legs. Was he this huggy here all the time? Must be a bit awkward in this undemonstrative crew.

Nathaniel and Blake held out chairs for Riley and her — a little shocking— and the guys took their seats. Blake prayed a thanks for the meal, and they all reached for the heaping bowls in front of them.

Dakota dared a peek at Declan, but he was ignoring her. Perfect. Toby had been right. Cook's meatloaf, mashed potatoes, and green beans were fantastic. Certainly better than anything Dakota would have found in her fridge or even on the menu at the Golden Grill, not that she'd tell Sage that, since her parents owned Jewel Lake's most popular diner.

"Travis says Toby will be attending preschool at Creekside Academy this fall?" inquired Kathryn.

The thirteen-year-old twins, Emma and Alexia, raised their heads. "Not fair," mumbled Alexia.

"We want to go to school," added Emma.

Kathryn glanced at her husband. "We live too far out of town for that to be practical. Plus, I'm an accredited teacher."

"Um, yes. I've got him enrolled for August. He'll like it better than nine hours of daycare." Single moms who worked for a living didn't have a lot of options, even with child support. If Dakota married Travis — not that the offer would be accepted even if presented —

she could afford to sit around at home all day like Kathryn.

Was that what had driven the widow to accept Declan? They'd each had three boys when they'd joined households years ago. Maybe Kathryn had been tired of single-momming it. She sure hadn't married the rancher out of love. Maybe out of pity for his kids.

Well, love wasn't in the cards for Dakota, either. She'd thought Travis was the one. She wouldn't have slept with him otherwise, and what a mistake that had been, linking their lives together forever. But Travis was too much like his father. Opinionated. Sour. Angry. As time went on, he'd covered up the softer sides she'd glimpsed until now, a few years later, she could barely remember what they'd been.

Drat the man. She'd loved him, flaws and all and, by golly, he had a lot of them. To him? She'd just been a conquest, no sooner won than discarded. Well, he was stuck with her now. And she with him.

The front door opened and closed. Boots scraped on the mat. And then Travis and Adam appeared in the doorway. Adam gave his wife a kiss on the cheek as he slid into the empty chair beside her. Travis — she was sitting in his seat. She started to rise, but he waved her back down.

"Don't worry about it." He dragged a chair in from the corner, wedged it on the corner between Declan and Ryder, and dipped his head for a quick prayer.

Huh. She hadn't thought his faith meant much to him these days. Didn't he only go to church because it was expected of him, which was a bit of a laugh since Declan didn't attend? It wasn't likely real, just a show Travis put on to make her wonder.

Then his gaze met hers down the table. "I've got good news and bad news."

Uh oh.

"Your gas tank is topped up." He shoveled in a bite of meatloaf.

"Thank you."

"But your fuel pump is shot."

"My... what?"

"Fuel pump. The sputtering wasn't because of low fuel but deliverability. The fuel pump sends the pressurized gas from the tank to the engine." He scooped mashed potatoes into his mouth.

She waited until he looked at her again. "So, I need to make an appointment with a mechanic?" And how much was that going to cost? Maybe she could get her brother to help. Or probably not.

"No." In went some green beans. This kept up, she was going to hike around the table and grab his fork. "Adam and I shoved it off the edge of the road. I'll go into town in the morning and grab one for you. It'll take me a couple of hours to replace it."

"But I..."

"Sorry if you've got a hot date tonight. You're not going anywhere."

"But I can't stay here!" Not that she hadn't before, but there was no way she was stepping foot in Travis's cabin that way again.

"We have a spare room." Kathryn rested her hand on Dakota's arm. "It's no trouble."

"But..."

"Goats butt," said Alexia with a giggle.

Everyone turned to glare at her.

She tossed her blond hair over her shoulder. "Well, *I* thought it was funny."

"It wasn't." Her twin rolled her eyes.

"One of the girls can loan you pajamas, and there are some unopened toothbrushes in the upstairs bathroom. You'll be just fine."

Dakota would *not* be just fine. "How about I borrow your truck tonight, Trav, pick up the part in the morning, and bring it out here?"

Travis shook his head. "It's loaded with all the fencing supplies. Sorry."

Dakota looked around the table, but everyone seemed quite focused on finishing their meal. Great. No one was going to come to her rescue.

She was stuck.

CHAPTER THREE

Travis rubbed his eyes and tried to move the hard, warm little body that angled across most of his bed. It might have been the worst night the kid had ever had since he'd learned to sleep through the night. Knowing his mother was over in the ranch house had turned Toby into a pathetic, needy mess.

There was a slight hint of dawn through Travis's uncurtained window. He might as well call it morning for all the good trying to fall asleep again would do. Dad had never allowed laziness so, even as a teen, Travis rarely had the luxury of sleeping in. Up and at 'em early was habit.

Didn't mean his son needed to be up yet, though. Travis slid out without dislodging Toby then tucked the duvet around the boy. As always, his heart seemed to expand at the sight of the tousled dark hair, the long lashes fanned across round cheeks, and the arm thrown over his head.

How could something so perfect, so beautiful, come out of the toughest time in Travis's life? As much as he'd been sorry for the way their son held him captive in Dakota's life like burrs spiked into tender skin, he still couldn't completely regret their promiscuous nights when the future seemed golden.

He and God'd had a few discussions about the dichotomy there. Somehow, Travis was able to love and appreciate his son fully while regretting the circumstances of his conception. It didn't make sense, but it didn't have to.

Travis flipped on his coffeepot, took a quick shower, and poured a mug. He carried it out to his camp chair on the narrow front porch, pulled out his phone, and began to read his daily devotional.

He took a sip of his coffee then let his gaze unfocus from the corrals across the lane and the mountains beyond. The people of Israel had screwed up at least as often as Travis had, but God offered them another chance, over and over, just like He'd done with Travis.

If only it was as clear what Travis should do about the mess in his life. The Israelites had clear directions. They knew exactly why their life was snarled up.

That part, Travis knew, too. But he had less clarity than they did on where to go from here. A flaming pillar or a fluffy beckoning cloud would be mighty appreciated about now.

"You're up early."

Travis sloshed his coffee as he focused on Dakota standing in the lane not ten feet away. How had he not heard her approach? "Always. Besides, Toby wouldn't settle down last night and wound up in bed with me."

She frowned. "Is that typical?"

"Not at all." He hesitated. "It also isn't normal for him to know you're only a couple of hundred yards away."

"He wanted me?"

"You don't need to look so happy about it."

"Good grief, Travis. You act like a bear coming out of hibernation. Relax for five minutes. Smile. It might earn you a friend or two."

Who needed friends when he had brothers? But the flip side was, who needed enemies when he had brothers? He once would have put Adam firmly in the enemy camp, but the guy had mellowed a lot over the winter. Riley's love had been good for him.

That was Travis's problem. No one loved him but Toby. Not really. And while the unconditional love of a small child filled empty spots Travis hadn't known existed, it didn't replace the desire to be loved like Riley loved Adam.

"Sorry." Dakota sighed. "I wasn't trying to offend you."

An apology from his ex? That was new. "You're not completely wrong about the bear part."

She huffed a laugh then her gaze took in his phone. "Checking your email? I thought you didn't have WiFi out this far."

Who'd email him, anyway? Travis shook his head. "Bible reading, actually."

If her eyebrows shot up any further, they'd pop the cowboy hat off her head. "Really?"

"Why would I lie about it?" He tapped to revive the screen then held it out to her. "Right here if you want to see."

"Um, no, that's okay. Where are you reading?"

"Kings and Chronicles. I'm doing a one-year chronological plan."

Dakota opened her mouth and snapped it shut.

"I might be a grumpy grizz of a guy, but give me credit for trying."

"Just surprised me is all. I thought you only went to church because it was expected of you."

He rolled his eyes. "I'm an adult, Dakota. My father isn't going to kick me off the ranch if I don't go to church. It's not like he attends, so he could hardly hold it against me. Truth is, I'm working to change. To be a better man. I've told you that before, and I didn't say it to get on your good side." Not that it would have worked, anyway.

"Full of surprises today, Travis Cavanagh."

"Glad you noticed." And what was one more? "Can I get you a coffee? Cook won't put on a pot for at least another hour. I don't have any girly creamers, though."

"Thanks. Black is fine."

Drink it black. It'll put hair on your chest. Grandpa's challenge came to mind unbidden as Travis went through the door. He definitely didn't want to think about hair on Dakota's chest. Shouldn't be thinking about that part of her body at all.

He poured her a mug, topped his off, and listened for Toby. Still quiet. Then he went back outside and handed a cup to Dakota. She lowered herself to his top step, and he settled back into his chair.

"Thanks."

"You're welcome." Listen to that. They could address each other politely, after all.

"What time is the auto-parts store open?"

"Not for a good three hours yet."

"I'll hang out with Toby while you drive in."

"No." So much for civilized.

"What do you mean, no? It's a long trip for him, and you'll be in town for what, ten minutes? It's better if he stays here with me."

"Not a chance, Dakota. You might have forgotten, but it's the weekend, and that makes it my time with him. Just because your car broke down up here doesn't negate that."

"You make it sound like I sabotaged it on purpose." She glared at him, hard.

Now they were back on familiar footing. It shouldn't be a relief, but it sort of was.

Travis tipped her a look. "Didn't you? Convenient timing."

She surged to her feet and dumped the coffee on the grass. "Don't even start. I'll call roadside assistance. I don't need you."

He unclipped her keys from the carabiner on his belt loop and twirled them. "I don't think so, sweetheart. I'm going to fix your car, whether you like it or not. And Toby stays with me."

Dakota plunked the empty mug down on the top step, shot him a furious glare, and stalked away.

He watched her until she rounded the curve toward the ranch house. He'd won that bout and managed to get them back to familiar ground. Because a softer Dakota who wanted to probe beneath the surface about his faith made him too vulnerable.

Travis didn't dare let her in.

DAKOTA BRUSHED Toby's pony until her coat shone. She knew her way around the Rockstead stables from all the time she'd spent at the ranch in years gone by. Since she didn't want to hang out with Travis — controlling jerk — and he wouldn't let her near Toby, this was the best spot. She definitely didn't want to stay in the guest room or any place the girls, Declan, or Kathryn might see her.

At least Clover was happy to soak up some attention in exchange for a few carrots.

"Hi, Dakota. Wow, Clover looks good."

One of the twins. Dakota could never remember which was which, though they weren't identical. "Thanks. I needed to kill some time."

"Breakfast will be in just a few minutes. Might want to wash up."

"I'll skip it, thanks."

The girl snickered. "How can you manage without breakfast? That's crazy. Besides, it will be good. On Saturdays, Cook makes pancakes with berries on top 'cause Toby loves them so much. Truth?" The teen leaned closer. "They're Alexia's and my fave, too."

So this was Emma. *Brilliant deduction, Sherlock.* Dakota's resolve faltered. She rarely missed, because Toby woke up starving. If she fixed food for him, she might as well eat, too. There might be a box of crackers or a protein bar stashed in her glovebox. Right, and Travis had the keys. "Okay. You talked me into it."

The airhorn blasted, and Dakota jumped. "How can you live with that?"

Emma shrugged. "You get used to it. And you can hear it from probably three miles away, so you always know when it's mealtime."

Dakota washed up in the stable's sink and followed Emma to the house, where Toby grabbed her hand and gave it a swing. She'd lift him and give him a hug if it weren't for Travis's dark gaze. She was on his turf, and she wasn't welcome. Fine then.

She let Toby drag her toward the table then listened to Travis pray a short grace over the meal. Something she'd never thought would happen.

If he'd changed, why was he still such a grouch? It didn't make sense. He'd probably faked reading his Bible this morning just to lull her. She should've taken him up on the offer to see what app he had open.

Dakota took Riley's invitation for a ride after breakfast, where she managed to keep the conversation turned away from Travis.

The ranch was gorgeous in mid-June, with all the trees in leaf and fragrant wildflowers in the meadows. After a while they circled around to the lane where Travis was lifting off her car's back tire. Then he squatted to set a second jack underneath.

Riley took Dakota's reins as she dismounted. "See you back at the house!"

Not if Dakota could help it. She'd turn around right here and drive to town. But for now, Toby came running toward her. "Hey, buddy." Travis couldn't fault her for picking him up. Not when the car was up on blocks, and safety was a factor. She squeezed her son tight. "What's Daddy doing?"

"He has to fix it."

"Does he know how?" Dakota noticed Travis's shoulders tense then relax again. Those shoulders, so strong. She remembered the feel of them under her roaming hands and shuddered. No going there.

"Daddy know everything."

At least, he pretended to. But that wasn't fair. He kept a lot of the equipment running on the ranch, tractors and balers and such. Of course, he knew how to replace a fuel pump.

She watched as he emptied the fuel tank into a jerry can, reveling in the feel of her son's arms squishing her neck while she focused her gaze on her ex's flexing muscles. Not something she could usually get away with.

Travis deftly removed a small cylinder and replaced it before putting the pieces back together. He poured a small amount of fuel back into the tank before climbing into the driver's seat to test the repair. When the car started right up and he'd listened a minute, he nodded and shut the engine off.

It took only a few minutes to put the wheel back on, lower the car to the ground, and refill the tank. Travis lifted the tools into the back of his black pickup and wiped his hands on a greasy rag before meeting her gaze. "All done."

Toby wiggled to get down, so she let him. He ran to Travis, clapping. "Good job, Daddy!"

Dakota winced as Travis scooped him up with oil-covered hands. "Thanks, cowpoke. Just to keep you safe."

Not for Dakota, of course. It was all for Toby. Everything was. All the child support Travis paid, all the little things he did. None of it was for any lingering love for Dakota, not after the way they'd parted.

At least he didn't take his anger with her out on their son. No, Toby was the center of his daddy's universe, same as he was of his mama's. And those two universes were not likely ever to align. She knew that. She'd known it for several years.

Didn't stop her from wishing.

And wishing was something to squash down, way down, with never a hint to the outside world that Dakota had any regrets. Better that way, for Toby's sake.

For hers.

"I left your keys in the ignition." Travis's chin jerked toward the driver's door.

In other words, get out of his life and leave him alone with his son. Their son.

"Thanks." If her voice was a little rough as she slid into her car, he'd just assume it was residual frustration.

But it wasn't the kind he thought.

CHAPTER FOUR

H adn't seen Dakota for a while."

Travis faltered on his steps. He'd been so deep in thought he hadn't even noticed Blake sitting in his camp chair on the deck. Not good for a cowboy to be so distracted. Not when bears or coyotes or even wolves could surprise him at any time. "Hey."

Blake was the next brother to him. Full brother, that is, since Kathryn's twins, Noah and Nathaniel, came between them in age. Travis and Blake had never really been close. Travis had been shoving nearly everyone away for years, long before their father had married Kathryn.

"Kind of weird having her up at the ranch?"

"Duh." Travis eyed his door. He'd practically have to trip over his brother's stretched-out legs to get inside. Maybe he should talk a few minutes. Preferably not about Dakota, though.

"She couldn't keep her eyes off you." Blake chuckled.

"You're delusional."

"You are."

"Seriously, dude. If she looked my way at all, it was only to be sure Toby was okay. She's not used to seeing us together."

Blake shook his head. "Give her the benefit of the doubt for five seconds, Trav. She's a good mom. You once had a thing for her."

And never gotten over it.

Travis parked on the top step, right where Dakota had sat Saturday morning. "Doesn't matter. I might've once loved her, or thought I did, but it didn't last. And it's not surprising."

"Because you're such a grump?"

"Gee, thanks, little brother."

"I'm serious. Lighten up a little. Laugh once in a while. She wouldn't be able to resist your charm if you showed you had some."

"What makes you think I want her back?"

"Don't you?"

Travis let that hang in the air for a few seconds, pretending to think about it. "Even if I did, which I'm not admitting to, it's not that easy. Because you know what? I'm not worth hanging around for. Learned that with Mom, and Dakota drove it home after Toby was born."

"Our parents' divorce wasn't on us boys, you know. Mom was psycho. She didn't act like a mother."

"Because we weren't worth being her sons. What kind of parent could walk away from lovable kids? Toby... I could never do that to him."

"Watch who you're calling unlovable. I'm not gonna wear that label."

"I don't see you beating down some woman's door with your undying love."

Blake shrugged. "It'll come. At least I don't have it just beyond my fingertips where some genuine remorse might show her Mr. Nice Guy isn't just an act."

"Get a life, Blake. If she thinks of me at all, she's either worried about Toby or she wonders how she was ever stupid enough to fall for me in the first place. She thanks her lucky stars every day she's not stuck with me."

"Lucky stars? Thought she was a Christian."

Travis waved his hand. "Use whatever term you like. She's told me enough times she doesn't want to spend an extra minute with me. She dates other guys all the time. If she loved me, she wouldn't do that."

"Oh, like you're a heavy dater yourself. You just like people to think you are."

"If she can do it, so can I."

"Dude, do you even hear yourself?"

"What's that supposed to mean?"

"Maybe you guys deserve each other, right the way things are." Blake rose out of the canvas chair. "You're like talking to a brick wall. You've got a big mural painted on your side of it and have convinced yourself it's reality."

Because it was.

Travis stood and faced his brother. "Want to know something?"

"Will it make me think you're less of a jerk than I think now?"

"Don't you remember how it was when Mom left? Wouldn't it have been better for us kids if they'd just tried to get along and not fought all the time? I hated trying to fall asleep listening to them yell and cuss and throw things."

Blake took a quick glance around and lowered his voice. "Pretty sure Dad wasn't any easier to live with than Mom was."

"I think Mom did the throwing."

Blake shrugged. "Probably. I don't remember her much. Not like you do."

"Here's the thing. I may be a lousy human being, but I love my kid. I'm his dad, and no one can replace me. I'm never going to walk away from him like our mother did to us. Never."

"I get it. I do. But wouldn't it be better if—"

"No. It would not."

At Blake's hiked-up eyebrows, Travis carried on. "Don't you understand? What we are doing works for Toby. So long as Dakota and I don't spend any time together, we're not going to fight. If we don't fight, Toby's world will stay right-side-up, and he'll turn out a normal human being. Even if Dakota gets hitched sometime, I'll still get him every weekend until he's eighteen."

"It wouldn't bother you if Dakota married some other guy? You're more messed-up than I thought."

Travis shrugged. "Why should I care?" Except even the thought felt like being disemboweled by a grizzly. "She's a free agent. She reminds me of that often enough. No, it's all about Toby, and that's all it can ever be. I'm not going to mess up his world, get his hopes up, and then wreck his life when it doesn't work out. Because it wouldn't work out, not for long." If ever.

Blake looked him eye-to-eye. "You really believe that?"

"Absolutely."

"You think our lives would have been better with Mom here, resenting every minute of it, but not fighting back?" Blake snapped his fingers. "Oh, wait. We've seen how that plays out. Her name is Kathryn."

"At least Alexia and Emma's parents stayed together!"

"Come on, man. You think the twins don't feel all the tension between our dad and their mother? They're thirteen, not stupid. If I were Kathryn, I'd walk. Dad's made all the same mistakes the second time around as he did the first. The only difference is that Kathryn isn't the same personality as *our* mom. I don't know if it's better or worse. All I can say is, it's different."

"And everyone tells me how I'm so like Declan." Travis shuddered. He sure had his dad's temper.

Blake got within an inch of Travis's face. "You don't have to believe it. You don't have to live it."

"I'm who I am, dude. And maybe it's best if Toby doesn't have to live with me seven days a week, fifty-two weeks a year. Maybe this way, he won't turn out like me."

"Do you even hear yourself? You think Dakota's brother and father are better role models? Not a chance. Scotty's a Class A jerk. Ask Riley if you don't remember."

Travis knew. Riley'd been sucked into Scotty's vortex when she'd been hitchhiking and he picked her up. Adam might have rescued her from the lout, but Scotty hadn't given up easily. He hadn't fully believed Riley loved Adam until their wedding a few months ago.

"If you really want what's best for your kid, do everything you can to patch things up with his mother. You don't have to be like Dad. You're a Christian. He's not."

Blake had a point in there, but Travis wouldn't ever admit it.

"I'm sorry, honey. You can't drop off Toby tonight."

"Okay, thanks." Dakota ended the call and huffed out a breath.

Her employee gave her a sympathetic smile. "No dice on your mom, huh?"

"Usually means Dad or Scotty is on a rampage." Dakota hated to admit to anyone how far from perfect her family was. Being a single mom was hard enough with support, but with her situation like this? Even harder.

"You know I'd watch him if I could."

"I appreciate the thought." Felicity had come through a couple of times in a pinch, but not often. "I'll just keep him here with me. It won't be the first time." Toby got so bored at the store these days. It was a lot easier when month-end landed on a weekend and he was with his dad. Then she didn't need to worry about him.

"Maybe your ex can pitch in."

How did Felicity guess she was thinking of Travis? Dakota shrugged. "Not possible. He lives too far out of town." She gave the girl a smile. "Don't worry about me. We're not your responsibility. Have a good time tonight."

"If you're sure."

"Of course." What else could she say? Pete would flip a switch if she billed him for extra hours for Felicity. He wasn't exactly an easy boss, and Dakota was on borrowed time if she asked — again — if she could wrap up June's paperwork on the weekend. Today was the thirtieth, and he expected the updated files in his inbox tonight.

Maybe Dakota should look for a new job.

But what? This managerial position paid better than most things she was capable of. Her parents hadn't been able to afford to send her to college, and she hadn't qualified for any scholarships. Nor had she cared back then.

It wasn't until after Toby's birth when she and Travis split up that she perceived her reality. No education plus a child meant her options were slim. Maybe when Toby was in school full-time, she'd start taking online classes. These days, she was exhausted by the time she tucked her son in bed.

She drove over to the daycare, the last parent to collect her kid again. Then over to the Golden Grill for their takeout order. Then back to From Stetsons to Spurs.

"Here we go, buddy."

Toby's lower lip protruded. "I want to go home."

"Me, too, but Mama has to work for a while yet."

"I want Daddy."

"Not tonight, buddy."

"But I want him."

"Sorry. You can watch Toy Story on my tablet." She opened her car door and grabbed the bag of takeout while Toby unbuckled his straps.

He stood beside her, arms crossed. "On your laptop."

"Sorry. I need the laptop." Dakota reached toward him, but Toby snatched his hand away like she was poison. *Thanks, buddy.*

"I don't want a burger."

"That's what you always ask for."

"I don't want it. I want meatloaf and gravy."

Like the Rockstead cook made. "I'll ask you next time. Tonight, it's a burger and French fries."

At least he followed her into the store's back door, where she set him up at his little table in the play area with the tablet propped on its stand.

What kind of lousy parent did this to her kid? No wonder he wanted his dad. Travis could take the weekend off and spend all the time in the world with him. Travis could take him riding and do all the cool stuff. In town, their son got dragged to daycare and then ate takeout in front of a movie he'd seen a hundred times while his mama worked some more. *Nice life, buddy. Sorry.*

She should stop apologizing to Toby and to herself. She was doing the best she could.

Her phone buzzed with a text. Mom was at the back door?

Dakota frowned and went to unlock it. "Hi! What's up? I thought you couldn't watch Toby?"

"Not at the house. Your father…" Mom shook her head. "But I can hang out with him here a while."

"Okay, thanks. I just put a movie on for him."

"Grandma!" Toby ran over and squeezed Mom around the hips. "I missed you!"

Mom wasn't one to make a fuss over the movie or the takeout. Dakota hadn't been raised much differently, even though her parents were together, unlike Toby's.

But there were assorted definitions of together. Declan and Kathryn were *together*, too, and no one was fooled into thinking they had a functional marriage. Dakota's mom put up with Dad's and Scotty's drinking and everything else because she didn't stick up for herself. She didn't expect anything better.

At least Travis wasn't a drinker. No, his temper had a way of flaring even without alcohol fanning the flames. That night she'd left… yeah, it had been bad. He'd been so angry with her he'd slammed a kitchen chair against the log walls of his cabin. The thing had shattered right along with Dakota's resolve to stick it out. If he ever turned to booze, there'd be no damper on his fuse.

That didn't jive with the guy who sat out on his deck in dawn's early light reading his Bible. Had he only been pretending?

Dakota couldn't take the chance. Dad had gone to church for a while when she was little, too, but he'd stopped a long time ago. If a man only did it to keep his woman off his back, it wouldn't last.

Was that really Travis's motivation? It didn't seem so. It also didn't seem to get to his heart, because wouldn't Scripture soften his attitude? It sure had for Adam, who used to be totally full of himself.

"Are you going to stand there and stare all night? Because I can only stay an hour, or your dad will wonder where I got to."

Dakota blinked. "Um, yeah. I'll get the cash register pulling all the June data right now. Sorry."

Another person she kept apologizing to. Nice.

CHAPTER FIVE

Travis hesitated, his fingers on his phone. Dakota was going to kill him, plain and simple. Still, Toby was his kid, too. Didn't that mean he could make some decisions himself?

But not without consulting her. Or, at least, telling her. No, consulting her. Wednesday was during her time, not his. He needed her to agree... even though he wasn't planning to back down.

Tricky.

He hated talking to her. He hated texting even more, since his fat fingers never hit the right letters and then autocorrect had a heyday and it was a royal pain to get the message right. And this would likely be a long conversation.

He'd call.

Or it could wait until Friday — except, no, it couldn't. Not when the first riding practice for gymkhana was before then. It was just an innocent set of horseback games for kids. Toby rode Clover for hours every weekend at

Rockstead. Alexia and Emma let Toby practice barrel racing with them. Sure, it was a girly sport, but the local gymkhana let little boys participate, too. It was good experience. Entry level.

Toby would love competing.

Dakota would hate it.

Wouldn't she? She'd loved the events as a kid and teen herself, but she was different about stuff in the past few years.

Travis tapped her number. Maybe she'd shunt him to voicemail.

But, no, she answered. "Trav."

Here went nothing. Travis took a deep breath. "Hey, I've got something I want to run past you."

"Oh?"

"So it's about gymkhana on—"

"No."

"I already signed him up for the weekly practices."

"Unsign him."

"No. He wants to. There's a tot category this summer, and Emma and Alexia are coaching him."

"While you pawn off your responsibilities."

She knew how to get to him, every single time. "While I'm right there watching him, actually. Think what you might, but I don't use the twins as free babysitters."

"Right."

Travis could practically see her eyes roll from thirty miles away. "Practices are Wednesdays at four. I know you're at work and he's at daycare then, so I'll pick him up and take him. He's pretty excited."

"You told him already, before you talked to me?"

Guilty. Travis rubbed the back of his neck. "It came up in conversation."

"You can't just do that, Trav."

"Why not? He told me he went to a birthday party at his friend's house. You never asked me if he could go."

"That's totally different!"

"Is it? I don't think so. You're not his only parent. I get to have some say, too."

"But that's…"

Travis waited a few seconds, but she seemed out of words. "I know you like riding, too. We had a lot of great times at the fairgrounds when we were kids. Why shouldn't Toby experience that?"

"He's four."

"Uh huh. Your point is?"

"You can't just do this."

"Four o'clock Wednesday. Let the daycare know I'll be there for Toby. I'll trailer Clover down." He tapped to end the call.

And waited for Dakota to call him back in a huff. She didn't. Did that mean he'd won this round, or that she was gathering ammunition? She had two days to try to fight him, but he'd win. Toby was too excited for Travis to let the little guy down.

"You sure you don't mind closing up tonight?"

"No. It's fine." Felicity shooed Dakota toward the door. "Go have fun at the fairgrounds."

"I'm not planning to have fun." What Dakota was planning on was being there if her little boy needed her. What was Travis thinking, putting a preschooler in any sort of training for competition, even a kiddie one?

Not without his mama. And if his mama just happened to keep an eye on his papa, just to be sure, then that's how it would have to be. She'd admit to nothing.

At the fairgrounds, she spotted Travis's truck hitched to the horse trailer. After parking her car nearby, she followed the sound of clopping hooves and laughing kids to the grandstand, where she leaned on the rail.

The twins darted around the arena on horseback, hair tied back under their helmets. At least Travis had brains enough to protect theirs. Then she spotted Toby, also wearing a black helmet, on Clover. He seemed to be listening intently to his dad, nodding every few seconds.

Then Travis smacked Clover's rump and stepped away. Toby led off at a trot, looking like he'd been born to it.

So much for pretending Dakota was here for her boy. Her gaze locked on Travis as she took a long inhale then exhale. Why on earth did he need to be such a hunk? He tipped his black cowboy hat down slightly, probably to keep the sun out of his eyes as he turned to watch Toby round the arena amid the mass of other kids warming up their mounts.

And then he noticed her. She could tell because he scowled, even though he kept rotating with Toby. Their son followed the twins through the barrels' cloverleaf pattern. One of the girls reached over to give him a high-five, and he beamed as he returned it.

Okay, so maybe Travis was right. A kid could thrive in

an environment like this. She had. It was also where she and Travis had first gotten to know each other. Dakota could only hope he was keeping a close eye on those half-sisters of his, or they'd be sneaking off behind the bleachers kissing some cute pimple-faced wannabe cowboys.

Like she had.

Dakota's chin came up as Travis waved their son over to the other younger kids before striding across the dirt toward her.

Long, lean, broad-shouldered, and hotter than a sizzling summer day. She took a deep breath and tried to match his scowl, but the sunny afternoon and the glee on Toby's face made it hard to stay angry.

"Hey." Travis hopped over the rail. "Didn't expect to see you here."

"Felicity offered to close up so I could come."

He offered a sharp laugh. "You don't trust me, I see."

Sometimes he made it so easy to clutch her grudges tight. "Or maybe I just wanted to see for myself. Ever think of that?"

"Oh, yeah?"

How long would it be before Toby sensed the animosity between them? Kids didn't miss much. His parents could do better. They *should* do better. "Trav?"

He looked at her, dark eyes hard. "Yeah?"

"How about we call a truce?"

His eyebrows shot upward. "Truce? Makes it sound like we've been at war."

Dakota bit her lip. "It feels like we have been. Toby deserves better."

"I'm not sure what you think a truce would look like. It's not like—"

"I don't mean dating or anything like that."

"Good. Because that ship has sailed."

He was so quick to deny what they'd once shared. But he was right, too. Letting her thoughts veer that direction would only lead to more hurt, and there were three of them to consider. If it were just her and Travis, they could give it another try — oh, who was she kidding? It would dissolve into fierce, passionate arguing in no time at all. Or passionate something. Plus another round of regrets.

But... Toby. He was the reason they needed to pull their own emotions and animosity and history out of the mix. They needed to work in tandem parenting him, not vying for which one of them he loved more.

That would be Travis, anyway.

Travis leaned over the rail, hands clasped in front of him. watching one of the other kids ride the barrels. Then he glanced her way. "So, if it's not that, what exactly do you mean?"

He sounded so civilized it gave her hope.

"Finding projects to do together, I guess. Making sure Toby knows we support each other as parents."

"Just want you to know I've never *not* supported you as a parent."

"Thanks. I've tried to do the same."

Travis shrugged. "So, what needs to change?"

I need you not to be so grumpy all the time. So controlling. But saying that out loud would defeat the purpose. "I just thought..."

"Hi, guys!" A hefty woman wielding a pen and a clipboard stopped just across the boards. "Toby Cavanagh's parents, right?" She snapped her bubblegum.

Dakota took a step back.

"That's us," Travis said. "But we're not—"

"Perfect. We're asking all the parents to volunteer for this summer's fundraising. What can I put you two down for?" She looked expectantly between them.

"Can I just make a donation?"

Dakota elbowed him in the ribs. Trust Travis to want to buy his way out of personal involvement. He was the one who'd signed their son up for this. "What are the options?"

Travis scowled at her, but Dakota kept her smile pinned on the woman.

"Well, we need timekeepers for events. Someone to head up the bake sale on the Fourth of July. Someone else to..."

"Bake sale. Sounds perfect. We'd love to do that, right, Trav?"

"We would?"

"Remember what we just talked about?"

He closed his eyes and schooled his expression. "Right. Sure. Whatever."

"Okay, if you just put your email address here, I'll send you the information from last year's fundraiser to get you started." The woman handed over the clipboard.

Past Dakota would have written in Travis's info and snickered behind her hand. But the new Dakota was going to do better, not trying to pick a fight so she could feel superior when he rose to the bait. She printed in her own email address and passed the clipboard back. "I look forward to hearing from you."

Travis leaned to look around the volunteer as she moved off to her next victim.

Toby was riding. He sure wasn't going to win a record for speed, but he did maneuver the pattern around the barrels correctly, concentration clenching his little face tight.

He looked so much like his dad. Wasn't the first time she'd thought that, either.

Travis hollered, "Good job, Toby!" and pumped his fist.

Their son flashed his daddy a grin then guided Clover to the far side with the other little kids.

Dakota took a deep breath. "Looks like he's going to enjoy it." Nearly killed her to say it.

Her ex swiveled to look at her. "Can I get that in writing? Signed, dated, notarized?"

"Jeepers, Travis. And you wonder why we need a truce."

He studied her and shook his head. "You really mean it, huh?"

"Yeah, I do. My parents have been sniping at each other all my life. *Your* mom got tired of it and left. I don't want Toby scarred like we were. He's a good kid, Trav."

"Might be because you're a good mother," he mumbled as he turned away.

Seriously? "You think that?"

He managed a jerky nod.

"Well, Toby adores you. I can't imagine your dad taking the initiative and signing you up for stuff like this when you were little."

Travis shrugged. "He might have. I'm just like he is."

Dakota dared to rest her fingertips on his forearm. "You're not, Travis. I know you think you are, but you are ten times the man your father is." At least, she hoped that was true.

He stared down at her hand until she removed it. "Thanks. You don't know what that means to me."

"I've got a pretty good idea."

Slowly he straightened and met her gaze. "So, you want a truce, huh? To get along better, but no dating?"

She nodded. "Yeah. Basically." Except when this vulnerable side of Travis turned up, she'd say yes to a date in a heartbeat. But would this side stick around? Because if they started going out again and then broke up, Toby would be seriously messed up.

And break up, they would. There was almost no chance in the world they could make it work. Better to not even try and get anyone's hopes up. Like hers. Because she'd never been able to get Surly Travis out from under her skin in all the time since they'd broken up. How could she ever get Nice-Guy Travis out?

He pointed across the arena. "Alexia's riding Domino. She's good."

Dakota studied the girl's seat and the way she leaned and guided her horse. "She's okay. Not as good as I was when I was her age."

Travis quirked a grin in her direction. "No one's as good as you were."

"Don't forget it." He could put any meaning he liked behind those words. "I'm going around to talk to Toby then I'll head home and start supper for him. Unless you want me to stay so you don't have to swing by the duplex to drop him off."

"Whatever works for you."

His voice was emotionless, and any moment they'd been sharing dissipated in the wind. But that was just as well, because Dakota wasn't strong enough for too much camaraderie. For all she blamed Travis for being a grump, she was likely to be the one who broke the new truce, because getting along with him was going to give her fickle heart way too much hope for the future.

Hope she didn't dare allow. He seemed to have changed, but was it enough? Would it really stick?

CHAPTER SIX

Y ou're doing what?" Blake snorted in disbelief.

"You heard me." Travis scanned the brush for the missing cow and the calf she should have birthed by now.

"I'm not sure I did. You and Dakota are organizing a *bake sale*? You and the woman you love to hate... or is she the woman you hate to love?" Blake shook his head. "Dude, you don't even know how to boil water."

"I know how to make coffee. Anyway, I don't need to know how to bake anything. She's going to call the parents, and I'm going to help with setup and takedown and all that. I can sell brownies like nobody's business, and I can certainly make change."

"You're doing this because Dakota asked you to? I knew you hadn't given up on her."

Travis's patience ran dry. "I'm doing this for Toby. Not for her." He nudged Lancaster around the thicket.

"Sure you are."

"Put your money where your mouth is. Why don't you

bake something for the sale? The twins are in the group, too."

"I'll buy some of the treats. You don't want me in the kitchen any more than you want to be there yourself."

A memory of the Rockstead kitchen in better days came unbidden to mind. "Popcorn balls."

Blake reined in Zorro. "What on earth?"

"Mom used to make them. Remember? I bet the recipe is around here somewhere. Cook might have it."

"Those were good." Blake smacked his lips. "Not sure what that's got to do with your bake sale, though."

"Doesn't have to be baked. Just needs to be edible stuff that someone might want to buy."

"That counts us out."

"I don't think so. You helped get me into this mess. It's up to you to follow through."

"Isn't that a cow over there?"

Travis's gaze roved the area. "Pretty sure not. Don't change the subject."

"You know, I might just do that."

"Oh, yeah? Popcorn balls? Thanks."

"Because now I really want to hang around at your little fundraiser and watch you and Dakota fight your attraction. I hadn't realized how entertaining you could be until she was stranded here that weekend. Better than a sitcom."

"We've turned over a new leaf."

"Hallelujah."

"Not the kind you think, dummy. We're just going to try to get along better for Toby's sake. It's not like she wants to go out with me, anyway. She made that clear."

"Right."

Across the gully, Travis spotted Ryder and Nathaniel. He squinted, trying to get a better look at where they were headed. "Is that a calf in the brush?"

Blake stood in the stirrups and shielded his eyes. "Could be. Don't see the cow, though."

"I've got a bad feeling."

"Ditto." Blake nudged Zorro into a canter, and Travis followed on Lancaster.

A few minutes later, the four brothers looked down at the remains of a calf.

"Not much left." Ryder looked glum.

"Wolf?" Nathaniel suggested.

"Maybe." Death happened, but every loss was felt, even with as many head as they ran at Rockstead. Travis nudged the carcass with his boot. "We need to find the heifer and bring her in."

He imagined Dakota's grief if something would happen to Toby. Yeah, he knew it was different for a cow. They weren't capable of love like humans were, but still, he was glad Toby wasn't riding with him today. The kid didn't need to see this.

Nathaniel pointed east. "Ryder and I will head around this side of the ridge."

"We've got the other." Blake glanced at Travis. "Okay?"

"Sure."

A few minutes later, Blake shifted in his saddle and glanced over at Travis. "So, about Dakota and you not dating."

"Shut it."

"No, really."

Travis rolled his eyes. "Let's talk about your love life,

okay? Seeing anyone these days?" Truth be told, he didn't pay much attention to what his brothers did off the ranch.

"Not lately. But then I don't have as much history with anyone as you do with Dakota."

"You mean you haven't made a baby that you know of."

"Believe it or not, I haven't been sleeping around."

"Good. Somebody needs to be smarter than me."

"Yeah, Nathaniel's pretty shook up since Ainsley ghosted him last fall."

Travis had heard a rumor or two. If he was going to pay closer attention, it would be about one of his own brothers, not one of the steps.

"He was all set to propose, too."

"Were *they* sleeping together? Because that's just a trap."

"Not sure, but maybe? At any rate, he was a mess there for a while. Still kind of grumpy." Blake shot him a look. "Reminds me of someone else I know."

"Just a reminder we don't share a speck of blood with those guys."

"*Those guys* are our brothers."

"Actually, no, they're not. They're Dad's second wife's kids. Or, you could say, they're Dad's additional free workforce."

"Paid. If Adam and Nathaniel weren't around, he'd have to hire some other cowboys. Dad doesn't pay us half bad, especially with all the benefits."

Nathaniel's twin, Noah, wasn't around the ranch much. He'd taken some initiative a few years back, apprenticed with a farrier, and now drove a circuit around the region, shoeing horses.

"Just saying," Blake went on, "that I've learned a bit

from watching you and Nathaniel. Adam, too. I don't think I'm ever going to get married."

"Me, neither," mumbled Travis.

"You could if you wanted. Do a little work like with this bake sale, and Dakota will take you back. I'd be starting from scratch, and I'm not sure I'm ready to."

"You make it sound like all I need to do is snap my fingers. There's more to it than that."

"Dude. Whatever it takes, do it. Isn't Toby worth it?"

"Toby's exactly why it's *not* worth it."

"Huh? Try making sense."

"Because it would never work, not long term. And if he gets his hopes up thinking we'll be a real family, then he's going to be crushed. Right now, all he knows is spending weekends here and weekdays with Dakota. He doesn't know that's weird. It's just how his life is, right? There's no emotion involved for him."

"Emotion. Do you even know the meaning of the word?"

Oh, did he ever. He had way too many of them stuffed deep inside, festering. "You've never had feelings, Blakey?"

His brother snorted. "Now I've got my big brother back. If you can't deny it, make fun of it."

"Do not."

"Point made."

Drat. "Anyway, that's why I'm never going to make a move on Dakota again."

Blake raised his eyebrows. "Otherwise, you would?"

This was getting too close for comfort. "I thought we were talking about your lack of love life."

"Nope. Yours."

NO MATTER how Dakota tallied up the list, they were a whole lot of promises short of last year's sell-out table. They'd been assigned a decent location, too. She just needed to get more baked goods on the list.

Or do a bunch of baking herself.

But wasn't organizing the event supposed to be her contribution? Yeah, she could make a couple of batches of brownies, but the list was considerably more than two pans short.

Maybe Cook up at Rockstead would do some. Then Dakota thought of going through Declan to ask her, and her enthusiasm shrank away in fear. Kathryn, though... but the woman wasn't Toby's real grandmother. Still, the boy had given her a hug, so they must have some sort of relationship.

The teens had a different fundraiser planned, so it wasn't like Emma and Alexia also needed to ask for sweet treats. They'd help her, though. She'd catch them at the practice on Wednesday.

Dakota bounced her pen off the paper. Was she really going to switch her schedule around and attend every week? And if she did, would it be for Toby's sake, or because she wanted the excuse to see Travis?

Never mind that.

Maybe Mom would bake. Unlike Kathryn, she was at least related to Toby.

Dakota tapped her mom's number. It rang twice, then a male voice answered, "Dakota."

Her heart sank. "Hey, Dad. Is Mom there?"

"No, she's gone to the store," he snarled. "What do you need help with this time?"

"Just wanted to talk to Mom."

"Well, she's not here."

Dead airspace. He'd already hung up.

Why did Mom put up with him? Why did Kathryn put up with Declan? It was a sad day when the only woman she felt she could understand was Travis's mother. The woman had been strong enough to stand up for herself and walk away instead of staying squashed under Declan's thumb. She should have taken her sons with her, mind you... but maybe she thought she was doing them a favor. Three rough-and-tumble boys and a big ranch seemed like a good combo. Until you added in their father.

See, that's why Toby was best off the way things were. He loved the ranch, and that was great. Dakota wasn't going to deny him that, but she also wasn't going to abandon her son to the likes of the Cavanagh men twenty-four-seven. No, it was best if she and Travis kept their sniping away from Toby's ears.

But working together... hmm. She eyed the clock. Travis would probably be in from his workday by now. Their crazy airhorn would go off in just a few minutes for mealtime. Maybe he'd be within cell range.

She'd do it. She tapped Travis's number.

"Dakota?" He sounded a small amount happier to hear from her than her dad had.

"Hey, I have an idea."

"Oh?"

"I'm having trouble getting enough donations for the bake sale." Although she hadn't asked Sage yet. She scribbled her neighbor's name on her list. "I was wondering if you'd like to come over one day soon and have a baking day with Toby and me. We can freeze it until the actual day of the sale."

"Let me get this straight. You want me in your kitchen with a frilly apron on? When you know I don't know a thing about baking?"

She hadn't thought of the frilly apron, and the thought spurred a giggle.

"So, it's all a joke to you."

"No, not at all. Real men bake, too, you know. It's not just women's work."

"I know that. But I'm pretty busy out on the ranges. I only get the weekends off because of Toby."

Dakota bit her lip. This could go very right or very wrong. "I know. That's why I was wondering about Sunday after church. I know you and Toby usually go to the Golden Grill for lunch with your family, but maybe, just once, you wouldn't mind coming here? I'll fix some sandwiches, and we can bake a bunch of stuff."

"You want to encroach on my time with my son?"

"That's not how I was looking at it."

"How many people have signed up?"

She gave him the number. "Last year there were nearly twice as many. I just don't know who else to ask."

"I can ask Cook. I don't imagine Declan would make a ruckus."

Dakota had noticed Travis often talked about his father by name, but now wasn't the time to bring it up. "If you think it would be okay, please do, and let me know."

"All right. So, you seriously want me to come and bake with you and Toby on Sunday?"

If only his voice wasn't so bland. He was usually much easier to read than this. "I'd like that. Since we're getting along and all that. Plus, we're in charge of this thing."

"Okay. Just this once. Don't get it in your pretty little head that you can mess up my time with Toby whenever you feel like it."

Her mind blanked on the rest of what he said. Had he really just called her pretty? He once had told her that all the time, but she hadn't heard it in a while.

She hadn't been acting like it.

"Dakota?"

She blinked. "Yeah?"

"I asked if I can bring anything."

"Um, no, that's okay. Anything you'd like to make?"

"Oatmeal raisin cookies."

Her brain shot back to when they were dating. Those had always been Travis's favorite. "They're for selling, don't forget."

"Very funny, Dakota. We can make a few extra, don't you think?"

She couldn't help grinning into the phone. "Possibly. I've got to go." Mostly so she wouldn't turn into a nostalgic fool and tell Travis how much she missed the old days before everything went wrong.

Because there was no way he felt the same.

CHAPTER SEVEN

S orry it's not homemade bread like Cook makes."
Dakota set a plate with tuna sandwiches on the
table next to some cut veggies and quartered
apples. Toby's favorites.

Her son climbed into his booster. "Looks nummy,
Mama."

"Thanks, buddy." She dared a glance at Travis. Even
though she'd told him sandwiches didn't mean she hadn't
triple guessed herself and had to talk herself down from
trying to impress him with how good a cook she'd become.
Only the fact that the meal needed to be quick so they
could get on with the main event, baking for the
fundraiser, had kept her in check.

"Want a Coke?"

"Sure, if you have some. Or water is fine." Travis took a
seat around the back of the table.

She didn't usually buy pop, but with him coming over?
Of course, she had. She set a can of it beside the glass by his
plate before pouring water for herself and Toby. Then she

offered Travis an awkward smile. "Would you like to say the blessing?"

His startled gaze met hers. "Uh, sure."

Toby held out his hands in both directions.

Dakota covered Toby's hand and clenched the other in her lap, bowing her head.

"Mama, you gots to hold Daddy's hand."

She hadn't thought this through. Here at home, with just the two of them, it was simple. Did they hold hands around the table at Rockstead? Not that she remembered.

A quick glance revealed Travis's hand stretched toward her, palm up. She could object, but that was silly. Besides, it would be over in a few seconds.

But she nearly snatched her hand away on impact. The warmth, the solidness, the zing — all nearly too much. Still, by the time Travis finished his blessedly short prayer, she didn't want to break the connection. She also didn't want to give him or Toby the wrong idea.

"Speaking of bread…" Travis took a bite.

What was with the man talking around his food? "I got this at the bakery."

He nodded as he swallowed. "Not bad. Cook said she'd be happy to contribute ten loaves of sourdough to the bake sale. That okay?"

"Great. Tell her thanks for me." Dakota might buy one of those herself.

"Oh, Blake and I found our mom's recipe for popcorn balls and made a trial batch a couple of nights ago. They disappeared in about eighteen seconds flat, so I guess they were okay. We can do some for the bake sale."

Look at Travis taking ownership of the fundraiser.

Wow. It'd been a long time since Dakota felt like she had a partner in anything. This only extended to this one event for their son. She knew she had to keep that in mind. But still, she'd enjoy it while it lasted.

"We're making a quad batch of oatmeal raisin cookies first. I'll put you and Toby in charge of that." She turned to her son. "You let Daddy put them on the trays, though. We need them all the same size."

Toby nodded. "Daddy's job."

Dakota tweaked his nose. "You've got it."

Travis crunched through a carrot stick. "What are *you* doing?"

"Some no-bake cookies since the oven will be tied up with your cookies for quite a while. Then a triple-batch of butterscotch brownies." If her memory hadn't failed her, those were another of Travis's favorites.

"Sounds good. What's your favorite, cowpoke?"

"Chockit."

"Chocolate?" Travis laughed. "Are you your mother's kid, or what?"

Toby scowled and crossed his arms.

"What'd I say now?" Her ex looked perplexed.

"You questioned his parenthood."

"I… what?"

"Think like a four-year-old."

"Been a while."

Dakota ate the last of her sandwich. Just when she thought Travis was trying, he reminded her not to get her hopes up. She knew better, anyway. Bake sale only.

She tapped Toby's plate. "Finish up so you can help Daddy."

"Okay." He took a monster bite and nearly choked.

A few minutes later she'd tucked the remaining veggies in the fridge and stacked the plates by the sink. After wiping the table, she began setting out the cookie ingredients. "Please tell me you know how to follow a recipe."

Travis rubbed his neck and squinted at the recipe card on the table. "Kathryn did figure boys needed home-ec classes."

"So that's a yes?" Dakota arched her brows at him.

"It's a sort of yes. I may or may not have flunked that class. I didn't see the point. I was going to get married and let the little woman do all the kitchen stuff."

Married. The little woman. He was talking about her and the dreams they'd once shared. Dakota took a step away. "You do realize that we live in the twenty-first century, right? Women have jobs. Couples share chores. In fact, in some households, the men do most of the cooking because they enjoy it, or because they get home from work earlier."

"Interesting," he drawled.

Dakota's temper flared. She visualized storm clouds dumping buckets of water on the inferno. What she'd really like was to dump them on his head.

"If you'd like, you can move the mixer to the table and plug it in under the window. You'll want to do four single batches instead of quadrupling it. The machine can't handle it."

"Bright red mixer?" Travis eyed the behemoth and then looked at her. "Why should I not be surprised?"

She liked to bake. She'd splurged on it. So what?

"You don't need it for whatever you're making first?"

He unsnapped his cuffs and began to roll up his sleeves. "I can probably use a spoon if you need the machine."

She averted her gaze from the tanned, muscular forearms as they appeared. "I'm on the stovetop first. It's fine. Be warned that Toby likes to make the mixer go faster and faster until things fly out of the bowl."

Travis grinned. "We Cavanagh men love power and speed, right, cowpoke?" He held up his palm for a high five.

Toby smacked it. "We gots to wash our hands first, Daddy."

"Lead the way."

THEY HADN'T SNIPED at each other in hours. Being in Dakota's kitchen, baking together like a family was more fun than he'd anticipated, even though it seemed to take forever to get sixteen dozen cookies through the oven. He'd thought four batches meant four measly pans. Showed what he knew.

Eventually, Dakota had pulled a container of stew out of the fridge and heated bowls of it in the microwave. Not that they were super hungry with the amounts of cookie dough they'd ingested.

Now the pans of butterscotch brownies were in the oven, all three at once, while cookies covered the table in neat rows. Toby splashed in the tub down the hallway while Dakota washed mixing things in the sink.

"Hey, I can do that." He hip-checked her out of the way.

She blew a strand of hair off her forehead as she looked

at him. "I thought you'd be in a hurry to get back to Rockstead. I can handle it from here."

"I don't remember much about home-ec, but Kathryn stressed that the work wasn't done until the kitchen was spotless."

Dakota glanced around the kitchen, and the lock of hair that had escaped her ponytail fell in front of her eyes again.

Before he could think better of it, Travis reached over and tucked it behind her ear. "Go sit down." His fingertips tingled from the touch of her skin, and a sudden longing swept over him. He could take a step closer, hold her face between his palms, and kiss her like he hadn't done since Toby was a newborn.

He shifted a half-step nearer.

Dakota whirled away, grabbed her kettle, and filled it. "Good idea. Tea sounds great. Would you like tea?" She was all but babbling in her haste to get away from him.

It had been a lousy idea, anyway. He knew better. She'd flat-out told him she wasn't interested in dating him again. Having any hopes was dumb. Stupid. They were long over, and now they were just Toby's parents, trying to work together without traumatizing their kid.

"No, thanks. I'll clean up here and then head back up to the ranch." He stuck his hands in the hot, sudsy water and scrubbed a measuring cup, rinsed it under the faucet, and set it in the drain rack before glancing back at Dakota, standing there in the middle of her kitchen floor looking at loose ends. "Unless there's something else you need me for." A guy could hope.

"No. Nothing." Her answer was quick and sure, but she

didn't meet his gaze. "Turn the kettle off when it boils, would you? I'm going to get Toby out of the tub."

"Can I tuck — never mind." It was Dakota's house. Her routine. He didn't dare presume she'd be okay with him interfering any more than he already had. Sure, it had been Travis's day, but that would have ended by suppertime. Now he was firmly in her time slot with their son.

"Yeah, sure. He'd like that."

"Really?" Travis shot her a quick look. She was taking this truce much farther than he'd expected. He kind of liked this new relationship.

Could get you in a load of trouble, cowboy.

Yeah, yeah, he knew. Dakota had boundaries, and she'd make sure he didn't cross them. With any luck, the fact that he liked the truce would keep him in line lest he lose the progress they'd made.

He heard their voices down the hall as he washed the last few mixing utensils, Dakota's low and calm, Toby's high and excited, both of them laughing.

This was what life should be like.

Travis paused as he wrung out the dishcloth. He'd missed so much time with Toby and Dakota. Not that he'd skipped a weekend with his son except for that one time he'd had the flu. He'd been present for the crawling and the early steps and the potty training, even though he'd fought Dakota hard on that one. Those had been a brutal few weekends. At first, he'd been sure she was laughing at him behind her hand, but it turned out she knew what she was doing. Having Toby in control of his own elimination turned out to be worth it when Travis no longer had to change stinky diapers.

Toby wouldn't be such a good kid if Dakota weren't such a great mother, and she'd had to manage by herself around a full-time job.

Because Travis had scared her off in his determination to rule the roost his own way. He hadn't listened to Dakota, not really. He'd learned since then that pregnancy hormones were actually a thing, and he'd been a jerk. Especially when she'd burst into tears and he'd lost his temper.

No wonder she'd packed up their infant and moved back to Jewel Lake.

Yeah, he'd been feeling all kinds of pressure from his father, too. His brothers had been little better. Everyone made him feel like a snarly bear trapped in a pit.

Because he was. Or, had been.

Expecting her to live in that tiny cabin, surrounded by the Cavanagh clan, might have been his first mistake. Or, no. That had been sleeping with her without thinking of marriage. He'd done everything backward.

Dakota's laugh rang out from the bathroom as the gurgling sound of the draining tub covered Toby's voice.

Travis felt like a man crawling in the desert with an oasis wavering far on the horizon. Was it real or a mirage? The only way he'd know for sure was if he kept heading that direction.

The kettle's whistle pierced the air, and Travis turned to flip it off. He wiped the counter and the stovetop and the sink.

The thunder of little-boy feet bounded into the kitchen. "I's ready, Daddy!" Eyes bright with glee, Toby danced around in his Buzz Light Year pajamas.

Travis scooped his child up into his arms and gave the damp cheek a whisker-rub.

Toby smelled of baby shampoo with a hint of his mom's lavender.

"I'm ready, too, buddy." Travis nearly choked on the words. He *was* ready. The big question was twofold. Was Dakota? And what would he do if she wasn't?

Because Travis was finished with the status quo. He hadn't laughed or relaxed in who knew how long. Until today.

CHAPTER EIGHT

Y ou let Travis come over for the entire day?"
Mom's voice rose incredulously.

"Not all day. We each went to church in the
morning."

Mom stood in front of the counter in From Stetsons to
Spurs, shaking her head. "I hope you know you're playing
with fire."

Been there, done that, got the baby. It wasn't a scenario
Dakota needed to repeat, for sure. But she also wasn't the
same girl she'd been five years ago. Raising a baby alone —
mostly alone — had grown her up a lot. Driven her to a
deeper faith than she'd had before, certainly.

"Dakota—"

"Mom, we were in the kitchen baking cookies and
squares for the gymkhana fundraiser. We were not giving
each other googly-eyes and smooches, okay? It was all for
Toby, and he lapped it up like a kitten with cream."

"Now he's going to expect..."

Dakota raised her eyebrows at her mother. "He's four

years old. He's not going to expect anything. He's settled into a routine: five days at home and daycare, two days at the ranch. Why would he think anything would change just because of one cookie-baking day?"

Her mother bit her lip. "I want to go on record saying this is a bad idea."

"So noted."

"You don't need *two* children out of wedlock. Not with a daddy's boy like Travis Cavanagh."

Fury began to billow up inside Dakota. "I'm not pregnant. I'm not going to *get* pregnant. I happen to remember how that happened, and it wasn't from baking cookies."

Mom looked away, but her lips were still pursed.

"And Travis isn't a daddy's boy." Dakota should probably have left off that last bit.

"Sure looks like one from here," Mom snapped back.

"Declan and Kathryn own one of the largest spreads in Western Montana. It takes a lot of manpower to operate it. Why shouldn't Travis work for his father instead of someone else taking that job while he works in town? That seems kind of silly."

"You're back under his influence. I can hear it in your voice."

"Listen, God knows how hard I've tried not to badmouth Travis to you or anyone else in the past few years. I've failed at times, but that's been my goal. Toby needs a dad he can respect, and if I stay out of their way, they'll do fine."

"Baking cookies together isn't staying out of his way."

Dakota stepped off to the side and straightened hangers

on the rack nearby with trembling hands. "That was a one-time thing. We're both Toby's parents, and we were asked to head up this fundraiser. We're only trying to do a good job. Toby shouldn't bear the brunt of his mixed-up parents."

"Your dad and I—"

"You're who taught me this response, you know. You let Dad order you around and yell at you." And worse. "I've seen where that track has taken you. That's one big reason I refused to put up with it from Travis." She hadn't dared tell her mom the whole story, about the rage Travis had flown into that last night. How that had been overlaid in her memory of a night she'd seen her dad do something similar, only Mom had been partially in the way and suffered a broken shoulder and a concussion. Dad had been remorseful, of course, and promised it wouldn't happen again. Dakota wasn't sure if it had. She'd never peeked out of her room again when Dad had been drinking.

"At least we're *married*."

If she thought her mom would take her advice and move out, Dakota would pack every box. She took a deep breath and addressed the actual current conversation. "It's not like I didn't figure out we messed up, but it's not something I can undo. Nor, frankly, do I want to. Toby's about the best thing that ever happened to me, even if he's also what keeps me linked to Travis." Maybe especially because of that. At least, in the past week or so, she'd begun to wonder... which was not something her mother needed to know.

The door to the store jangled as it opened. Finally

someone to interrupt this heart-to-heart. Dakota was so over it.

Until she saw Mrs. McDiarmid, the receptionist at Creekside Fellowship. She could only be here as a busybody. From Stetson to Spurs sold nothing but western wear, and the woman wouldn't be caught dead in a pair of jeans or a snap-front shirt.

She gave her best welcome-to-the-store smile. "Hi, Mrs. McDiarmid. What may I help you find today?"

The woman looked between Dakota and her mom as though weighing her options. "Hi, honey. Hello, Wanda."

"Good afternoon, Melanie." Mom's voice turned positively frosty.

Good. Maybe she'd leave. Maybe they'd both leave. Was it wrong to hope that?

"I heard that Riley and Adam are expecting, and I hoped you could tell me if the rumor is true."

"I'm sorry." Dakota wasn't. "But I'm not privy to the Cavanagh family secrets, so I don't have any information." And if she did, Mrs. McDiarmid would be the last person to hear it from Dakota's lips. Why did Creekside Fellowship keep the woman on payroll, anyway? Surely the pastors knew she was a gossip.

"It's really none of your business," Mom muttered.

"Oh, I was only curious. There's no harm in that."

"You're spreading rumors."

Where was Mom getting this bravery from? If only she'd use it to stand up to Dad.

Mrs. McDiarmid chuckled. "No, no. This is called fact-checking. I wanted to be sure before I told anyone else, and

I knew Dakota would be just the person who could give me the information."

Dakota crossed her arms. "You're mistaken." About all of it.

"But I saw your cowboy's truck out front for hours on Sunday. Why, he didn't leave until past nine o'clock! I'm sure Toby was asleep long before then."

Mom gasped and shot a horrified glance Dakota's way.

"I'm not sure how you know that, since you live several streets away. It sounds like you made a few trips over to check on my virtue. I'd like to say I appreciate it but, honestly? I don't."

"You need to think about how it looks to your neighbors, honey. Especially when you've already borne Travis one child. People will be quick to believe it could happen again."

"You may leave now." Who cared if her boss found out she'd sent away a potential customer? Mrs. McDiarmid would never buy so much as a bandana here. Even if she wanted to, Dakota would let the competition take her money.

The woman shook her head. "I'm sorry you don't understand how people think."

Dakota took a deep breath. "And I don't think you understand how much the Bible has to say about those who gossip. Check the book of James, for starters."

She could quote chapter and verse, but then she'd just be malicious, no better than the woman in front of her. James 1:26 was sure a temptation, though. *Those who consider themselves religious and yet do not keep a tight rein on*

their tongues deceive themselves, and their religion is useless.
Yep, she'd keep that to herself for the moment.

And why did she know that verse so well? From trying
to learn not to snap back at Travis. Who knew that turning
the other cheek and trying to get along was the more effec-
tive response?

The chimes jangled furiously as Mrs. McDiarmid
stormed out of the building.

Now, if only Mom would leave, so Dakota could take
some time to analyze if she'd been rude or right. Sometimes it was a fine line.

THIS TIME, Dakota had arrived at the fairgrounds before he
had. Travis spotted her car in the shade, which wasn't an
option for a rig as long as his truck and horse trailer.

"Wait right here with Alexia and Emma while I unload
the horses, Toby."

"I know, Daddy." His son gave a long-suffering sigh.

"Good." He got the twins' mounts out first. They
saddled up and headed for the other teens while he tossed
Clover's saddle on and hoisted Toby up. The boy knew
where to go and trotted off.

Travis's chest swelled with pride. Awesome looking
little cowpoke, and it was more than skin deep. Toby sat
that pony like a pro.

Where was Dakota? Ah, over there talking to the
woman who'd roped them into the fundraiser. Travis could
kiss her, he was so thankful for the great day they'd had

together on Sunday. But maybe kissing the stranger would send the wrong signal.

He chuckled to himself on his approach, and Dakota turned toward him.

"Someone's in a good mood."

"Sure. Why not?" He shrugged.

"I can tell you ten reasons."

Uh oh. She looked annoyed. What had he done this time? He couldn't think of a thing, unless she was dredging from much further back in time. He'd behaved lately. Hadn't even tried to kiss her goodbye the other night, though the temptation had been mighty strong. She'd been so pleasant to be around and had even talked to him like a civilized person over a cup of tea after Toby had ridden off into dreamland.

He looked at the volunteer coordinator then back at Dakota. Best not to mess with whatever was going on. She'd tell him, or she wouldn't. He jerked his chin toward the rail. "I'll watch Toby from over there."

A few minutes later, Dakota came over and stood beside him, but not as close as last week. "People are talking," she said quietly.

Travis angled a look her way. "About what?"

"You and me."

"I thought there wasn't a you and me. Did I miss a memo?"

"Don't be dense."

Okay, so Sunday had been an anomaly after all. But if it had happened once, it could happen again. He nearly snorted. Look at him, all optimistic and everything. Obviously, that attitude had to go… while not allowing himself to dip back into surliness. This should be a fun bronc to ride. "Pretend I *am* stupid and explain it to me."

"I'm not in the mood for this, Travis."

"You think I am?" Sue him if his bad attitude showed through. It was her fault. He'd been fine — happy, even — until she came along. When would he ever learn to control his own moods and not let Dakota dictate them?

"I'm going to sit over there with a couple of the other moms." She pointed up the bleachers.

They were forty-something mothers of teens. His eyebrows rose. "Do you even know them?"

"They've been in the store."

Of course, they had. "And are they some of the people who might get ideas if Toby's parents actually talk to each other?"

"Um, not them. Maybe. I don't know."

"That's all you've got for me, Dakota? Seriously?"

She stalked away, climbed the bleachers, and sat down by the women, who barely paused in their chatter to each other. Clearly, it was Dakota's idea to sit with them, not theirs.

Whatever. Travis swung to face the arena again just in time to catch the timekeeper's flag for Toby. The boy rode with so much concentration his tongue was caught in his teeth. Travis could only hope Clover wouldn't stumble and cause the boy to bite it.

The pony took the turns a bit wide, but then, Toby was just a little kid. He was doing pretty well.

Travis wanted to discuss it with Dakota, but he was back in her bad books, and he didn't even know how he'd gotten there this time. He rubbed his neck and glanced over, but she was cheering for Toby. As she should be.

"Travis?"

He turned to see the 4-H club leader. "Hey, Chad."

"Thought that was you." The other man poked his chin toward the arena. "That's your kid, right?"

"The little guy, Toby."

"He's got a good seat."

"Spends a lot of time in the saddle."

"You're sharing custody, though?"

"Yeah. But I ride with him a lot when he's up at Rockstead on the weekends."

"How old is he?"

"Just turned four."

Chad whistled. "Figured him for older."

"Nope. Too young for 4-H, if that where you're angling."

"A man could hope. Four, huh? Well, I hope you'll put him in when he's older."

"We'll see. Can't really plan that far ahead. Besides, Rockstead's a long way out of town." Also, he didn't have custody during the week. There were only so many days he could take off early and come into town. He really only got away with Wednesdays since he brought the twins down, too.

Chad looked up the bleachers. "Heard you and the boy's mom were patching things up."

Travis scowled at him. "Where'd you hear that? That's just straight-up gossip."

"Not true then?"

If this sort of thing was what Dakota had been referring

to, her attitude made more sense. "All I can tell you is it's none of your business."

The man narrowed his eyes. "No need to get huffy. It was just a question."

Travis raised his voice. "Still none of your business." His fists found his hips as he widened his stance, glaring at the man. He forced himself to take a deep breath. *Let it go. Let it go.* He pivoted and stared into the arena where Alexia was taking her turn.

"Those girls would do well in 4-H."

Good thing Chad had reverted to the original subject again, because Travis had been about ready to punch him. "They're thirteen, but they're not my responsibility."

"I never see your old man to ask him."

"Not my problem."

And that's how many things needed to stay. Travis needed to focus on his work at the ranch and on his son. He couldn't get too sucked into the hot and cold of Dakota or anything else. Cowboying. Daddying. The sum total of Travis's life.

CHAPTER NINE

Travis loved riding. He did. But he loved haying just about as much. Driving in circles on Rockstead's big hayfields in air-conditioned comfort, keeping an eye on the huge round bales expelled by the baler was satisfying. Running as many cow-calf units as they did year-round took a lot of feed. Smaller ranches without hayfields sold their calves in the fall to ranches who fattened up the beef for market. But, especially with the annex of Running Creek next door, Rockstead was well set up.

Running Creek Ranch had belonged to Kathryn and her first husband, Joe Anderson. After Joe's death from cancer, Kathryn had married Travis's dad, combining the raising of their six boys. Combining the two ranches at the same time.

Travis took a swig from his water bottle and geared the machine down to make the tight turn at the edge of the gully. He knew what Declan had gotten out of the deal. He'd found a mother and teacher for his boys, so he could go back to focusing on building up Rockstead. And controlling operations at Running Creek had likely been a large part of his plan.

No wonder Adam was desperate to get his hands on his dad's ranch. Travis'd do the same. Well, except for Adam's crazy plan to pretend to be engaged to Riley, thinking Declan would be more easily swayed if Adam proved he'd settled down. Had totally backfired when Declan found out it was only a ruse... and then backfired again when Adam and Riley actually did fall in love and get married.

Bully for Adam. Declan had been *this close* to signing Running Creek over to Adam, Noah, and Nathaniel, but he'd pulled back in all that mess of lies. Adam and Riley still lived in one of the dinky little cabins down the lane from Rockstead's home-place, and renters still lived in Running Creek.

Travis? He'd just as soon his stepbrothers got their way. Running Creek was a lot smaller. Let them have it. Then Travis, Blake, and Ryder wouldn't have to share the larger spread with Joe Anderson's sons. Made sense to him.

He glanced across the gully toward the modest house in the distance. A friend of Dakota's brother rented the home-place. Bet that stung Adam.

But the delight Travis had always reveled in when Adam failed had dissipated since his stepbrother had returned from the rodeo circuit last fall. Winning the all-around championship should have swelled Adam's head to the point of swaggering pride, but the prize had been soured by the death of a friend and competitor, Ace Desjardins. The experience had affected Adam deeply. Actually turned him into a nice guy.

Travis hadn't wanted Adam to be a nice guy. Being tempted to like his rival had never been part of his game plan. He preferred to hold hurts and insults close, nursing the injustices of life. How dare Adam be older than Travis, dislodging him from the status of firstborn Cavanagh son? Why had Declan given the Cavanagh name to Kathryn's sons? Why had Kathryn allowed it?

Questions no one seemed able to answer, and the only two people who knew — Declan and Kathryn — weren't talking.

It bugged Travis less than it used to. He had more important things to mull over these days, like Dakota's worry over what people might think of them spending time together.

Why not let people guess the truth?

Travis's foot slammed the machine's brake. It jolted before he caught himself and smoothed out the action.

Let people guess the truth? That assumed there was a truth buried in there somewhere.

Travis loved Dakota. He had ever since they were teens. She'd seen something in the taciturn kid he'd been and sweetened him up like nobody else ever managed... or cared to. They'd even taken their time arriving at intimacy. Not *enough* time, mind you, but a whole lot longer than his hormones had wanted.

He'd been pretty happy when she told him she was pregnant despite all the precautions they'd taken. He figured that was a good time to make things official, but she'd disagreed.

Well, no biggie. Sure, he'd been hauled off to church every Sunday for much of his life, but lots of their friends didn't bother with a wedding. What was a piece of paper if a couple was dedicated to each other?

Except Dakota wasn't that loyal. They'd had a big row when Toby was a few weeks old, and that had been the end of Travis's dreams. He'd insisted on weekend rights, and she'd tossed in his face that would work well for her, since she didn't get much sleep as the mother of a newborn.

It didn't take many months before he began hearing rumors of this guy and then another guy she was going out with on weekends while he cared for their son. Travis had pulled into himself even deeper than when his mom left. Deeper than when the Anderson brothers had become Cavanaghs.

So what was this spark of hope doing in his heart, thinking Dakota didn't hate him as much as he'd believed for the past four years? Was Toby all that tied them together, or was there more?

Inside Travis? Definitely more. The more she'd flaunted her lifestyle, the more she'd appeared to be doing perfectly fine without him, the more she'd sniped at Travis at every opportunity, the surlier he'd become. More and more like the spring bear she'd accused him of.

But — and here was a novel idea — what if she'd been protecting herself the same way he'd been doing? What if all they'd been doing this entire time was reacting, not acting?

Huh.

Oh, it was dumb to even think that. Running on that assumption could get a cowboy in a heap-load of trouble.

But sticking to the way he'd been doing things thus far definitely hadn't been working. Not until he'd agreed to her proposition. What did he have to lose by changing perspective?

Toby.

But if Travis tried and lost, not much would seem different to their son. They mostly kept from bickering in front of him... because they'd avoided each other. Dakota wouldn't go so far as to try to prevent Travis from seeing Toby, would she? Well, then, he'd see an attorney and have legal papers drawn. Besides, if she was really dating other guys, she'd still want to have her weekends free.

It was time to stop pretending that thought didn't kick him in the gut like a wild bronc. He could man up and lay things on the line. He could.

But did he have the nerve to test their fragile relationship?

"Mama? Where's Daddy?"

Dakota parked her car beside the stable. Travis's truck wasn't in its usual spot, and she spotted Lancaster in the corral. So, he'd gone off the ranch, right when he knew Toby was coming. She'd meant to create a little distance between them, not send him packing like a dog with its tail between his legs. Although seeing him face off with Chad a couple of days ago had reminded her of what Travis was capable of.

She pursed her lips. "I don't know, baby, but if he's not here, Emma or Alexia will be."

"I's not a baby."

"I know, but you'll always be Mama's baby." Especially

since she was unlikely to ever have another. "Get unbuckled, okay? And I'll grab your backpack."

"Woody there?"

"I'll show you." She'd never be that careless again. Getting stranded up here with a wrecked fuel pump had been the start of all this awkwardness. Sometimes it felt better than the way it had been, and then she slapped herself up the side of the head — mentally, at least — and remembered the long game: getting Toby to adulthood unscarred despite his parents and grandparents.

She met her son around the back of the car, showed him the plush toy in his pack, and took his hand as they went into the stable. She blinked a couple of times to adjust to the dimmer light and spotted Riley in one of the stalls, a wheelbarrow parked nearby.

"Hi, Riley. They've got you back on mucking out stalls?"

The other woman straightened and grinned. "Hi, Dakota. Hi, scamp. Yep. Suits me just fine."

Dakota would fight Declan every inch of the way if he tried that on her. Another reason she and Travis were better off separate.

"Where my daddy?" Toby demanded.

"Making hay bales. Want to ride in the tractor with him?"

"Yeah! But is loud."

Dakota opened her mouth in protest and snapped it shut again. She couldn't dictate to Travis how he handled things with Toby. It wasn't like it was actually dangerous. The cabs were fully enclosed and probably had A/C, unlike her old car. Toby would be fine. Bored out of his skull, but fine.

"C'mon. I'll take you down to where he's working. Grab a helmet."

Toby ran to a stool, climbed up, and unhooked a helmet that must be as heavy as him. He struggled but managed to get it on his head.

Riley reached down and buckled it before grabbing one of her own. Then she looked at Dakota. "Hanging around for a bit? I shouldn't be long."

"No, I need to get back to town. I'll just, uh, toss Toby's backpack in at Travis's cabin and head out. Be good for Daddy, buddy." She bent and gave him a kiss on the little bit of face she could find.

Riley set Toby in front of her on the four-wheeler and sped off, leaving Dakota standing in the Rockstead stables, Toby's pack hooked over one finger.

Was Travis really too busy to meet his own son? Or was he avoiding Dakota again? Wow, give her two Fridays of seeing his face, and she expected it all the time. How could he have guessed she wanted to talk here where there were fewer onlookers to judge?

She strolled out of the stable and down the lane toward the row of cabins nestled against the creek.

Such a beautiful spot this time of the year. Someone had mowed recently and trimmed around each cabin's steps. It had been a few years since Dakota had spent much time up here, and she didn't know who inhabited each of the six cabins now.

Cook lived in one of them, though, and didn't Adam's twin brothers, Nathaniel and Noah share one, since Noah was rarely at the ranch? Dakota saw his farrier's truck around Jewel Lake from time to time.

The fourth one was Travis's, so she climbed the few steps and tapped on the door, even though she knew he wasn't inside. She cracked the door open. "Travis?" But, of course, he didn't answer.

Dakota edged inside and couldn't help glancing around at the sparse, log-lined interior with its wood-burning stove. No fire today, not in the languid warmth of June. Down the short hallway sat a bath and two small bedrooms. She wasn't going there, for sure.

There was a tiny kitchenette tucked on one side with a small, round table and a couple of chairs. She narrowed her gaze and ran her hand down the one that had been repaired. Travis — or somebody — had glued the broken back, sanded it smooth, and refinished it. She could barely see the cracks.

She'd been crying. He'd lost his temper. The chair had hit the log wall right... there, where there was a small dent still visible. He'd yelled at her, his face dark and foreboding...

No more memories. Time to get out of here. Dakota's hands trembled as she hooked Toby's pack over that very same chair.

But then she spotted a book with a tasseled bookmark peeking out the top, lying above a spiral-bound notepad. A men's devotional? Really? So it hadn't all been an act the other day when she caught him reading a Bible app outside in the early dawn. Bad her, she'd suspected he was faking it, even though he'd spouted the name of the reading plan. It could've been made-up.

Her fingers twitched to open the notepad and see what

he'd written in there. Would her name appear? Did she want it to?

No. Toby's pack. That was all. She backed toward the door, still eyeing Travis's reading material. It wouldn't hurt if she snooped, would it?

But how would she feel if he did that to her? She'd flip out.

So would he, even though he'd probably never find out.

Definitely none of her business. She let herself out onto the small deck and clicked the door behind her before breathing deeply.

It was obvious she cared far more what Travis thought than she was willing to admit, even to herself. A thought she didn't wish to entertain, even now, especially with the flashback of the night she'd thrown her clothes together, gathered her infant son, and fled the ranch.

She'd taken a few steps toward the stable when she realized there was a horse and rider stopped in front of her. Big black horse. Big black cowboy hat. Declan on Diesel.

"What're you doing here?" The man's gaze was hard, ungiving.

"Just dropping off Toby's pack. Riley took him down to Travis."

"Did Travis give you permission to go in his cabin?"

"I had to put Toby's pack somewhere. I didn't touch a thing." Good thing she could say that with a clear conscience.

"Don't mess up my son or my grandson." He shifted ever so slightly in the saddle, but Diesel knew his signals and trotted off.

Dakota stared after the broad back of the middle-aged

rancher. The nerve of the man to assume all Travis's problems could be laid at her feet. Wasn't it clear that Travis was only reacting to the way he'd been raised?

It was up to her to break the chain for Toby and not let him grow up to be an uptight, angry man like his grandfather and father. She should be avoiding the ranch. Avoiding Travis.

CHAPTER TEN

Travis whistled as he looked around the booth. "Wow, where did all this food come from?" He slid Toby to the ground. "Your mama's been a busy woman."

Dakota turned to face him, adjusting the stick-things that held her bun in place. It looked like chopsticks, but he knew better than to comment. "Some of the other parents came through in the end." She squatted and held out her arms to Toby. "Hiya, buddy. Got a hug for Mama?"

He squished his mother's neck, but Travis could see the little guy wasn't into it. "Can I has a cookie, Mama?"

"Didn't Daddy feed you breakfast?"

He shook his head solemnly, and Dakota looked up at Travis, her gaze accusing. "He didn't eat?"

Travis laughed. "Think like a four-year-old."

She scowled. "What do you mean?"

"I didn't feed him. I didn't even make it. Cook made pancakes, and Toby ate them all by himself."

Dakota aimed a look at Toby. "Is that what you meant?"

He nodded vigorously. "Daddy not feed me."

She tweaked his little red cowboy hat. "Monkey." Then she put a hand to the edge of the table and rose to her feet.

"You okay?" She didn't look okay.

"I'm fine. You like the display? Sage found this old shelving unit in the back of the Golden Grill, and her parents said I could use it today. Good thing, because no way was everything fitting on that table."

"You should have called. I could have picked it up. You didn't need to haul that thing yourself." How could she even have done it? The boards were too long to fit in her little car.

"Dad and Scotty brought it over."

"Oh. That's good, I guess."

Toby clambered onto a folding chair and surveyed the spread on the table. "I want that." He pointed at a foil pan of cake with white icing covered in sprinkles.

"Not now, buddy." Dakota touched his arm, but he yanked away from her. "All this stuff is for people to buy, and then the money goes to the fairgrounds so kids can ride there."

Toby scowled.

"I could b—"

Dakota's gaze flashed to his. "Don't even start."

"Why not? Looks good to me, too. I'm happy to pay, so the end result is the same. Right?"

"No. Maybe later."

If there was any left, she meant.

She pursed her lips. "They'll be opening the gates any time now. Why don't you take Toby and see what there is to see?"

"You trying to get rid of me? I thought we were in this together."

She touched her hair again. Nervous, huh? "Toby will be bored, and it *is* Saturday after all. Your day."

"You *are* trying to get rid of me. What does it matter what people think?"

"Because they…"

"So let them."

She glanced at Toby then back to Travis. "It's not as easy as you seem to think. I live and work in town. You don't."

Travis shrugged. "Doesn't matter." Yeah, Chad's questions had bugged him the other day, but whatever. He wasn't going to let some random guy's opinion sway him one way or the other. Not when he'd decided to give Dakota one more chance. Of course, she didn't know that yet, and this wasn't the time to tell her. Or ask her. Or whatever a guy was supposed to do at this stage.

He rubbed the back of his neck. Yeah. It was complicated, and he could see that outside pressure wasn't going to be much help. Finally, he nodded. "Have it your way. What time do you want me back here so you can take Toby exploring yourself?"

"But it's Sat—"

"So? Is this a normal Saturday? No. We're at the fair for the Fourth of July, where there's tons of stuff to do. You want to be stuck at the bake table all day? I can take my turn. And you're right, our little cowpoke would be bored hanging around here all day. And probably try to talk people out of buying the treats he thinks he wants."

He was winning. He could tell by the softening lines

around Dakota's eyes and the twitch of her pretty pink lips. Without stopping for thought, he leaned over and pressed a quick kiss to her cheek. "C'mon, Toby. Let's go see the fair." He grabbed his son's hand and walked away.

Travis would do his best to ignore the soft gasp Dakota had uttered as he buzzed her face. In fact, if he could rewind life by thirty seconds, he'd never have been so brash. What had he been thinking, right out here in the middle of the Jewel Lake fairgrounds with their community pouring in to see the sights?

He hadn't been thinking, plain and simple. But he couldn't resist a glance back before the crowd closed around him.

Dakota stood staring after them, her hand pressed to her cheek. When she caught him looking, she pivoted a one-eighty, both hands at her sides. Had there been a pink flush to her cheeks? Maybe.

All he knew for sure was that little swipe had been in the wrong place and not nearly long enough. Maybe she'd let him do it right next time.

"WHOA. Did I see what I think I just saw?"

Dakota turned slowly to see Sage's approach. She straightened her shoulders and put on a bright smile. Sales mode. She could do this. "Depends on what you think you saw. Can I interest you in some cookies, squares, or bread? All proceeds go to benefit the junior riders."

"Only if you tell me why it looked like Travis Cavanagh was kissing you. In public."

"I believe kissing is when it is mutual and on the lips. This was neither. Looking for something sweet or savory?"

Sage grinned. "Definitely sweet, although I feel I'd be negligent if I didn't remind you that whatever reason you and Travis had for not sticking together after Toby's birth likely still stands."

Of course, it did. "I'm only going to say this once. It's none of your business."

Sage held up both hands in defense. "Fine. Don't say I didn't warn you."

Dakota scanned the crowd. Travis and Toby were long gone, and a few people were angling toward the bake table. "Duly noted. But there isn't anything to worry about."

She'd been holding herself aloof for four years. Protecting herself. Protecting Toby. Suddenly she wanted to rethink everything, but now was not the time or place. Drat Travis, anyway. Why had he kissed her?

Not a real kiss, of course. Just a moment between friends. Being friends had been her idea, and one of her better ones in recent memory.

"Okay, well, that cake looks good." Sage pointed at the one Toby had been eyeing. There were several more the same. Maybe Dakota should set one aside.

Sage dug into her purse for a few small bills then tucked the container into the bottom of a mesh bag. "Thanks. I'll enjoy that later." She'd no sooner moved to the next booth when Mrs. McDiarmid took her place.

Oh, please, no. If anyone in Jewel Lake should not have witnessed Travis's kiss, it was the Creekside Fellowship's secretary.

"Good morning, Mrs. McDiarmid. Would you like to support the junior riders today?"

"A loaf of that bread, please." The woman pointed at one from the shelving unit and began to flip through her wallet.

"Here you go."

"Thank you." The older woman leaned closer. "I'm sorry about the other day. I really shouldn't have said that."

Would wonders never cease? "No problem, Mrs. McDiarmid. You're forgiven." And Dakota might need to repent of her uncharitable response. "If you're ever looking for any western wear, please do stop by the store." As if someone who wore pantsuits from the eighties would find anything there.

A snide remark seemed on the tip of the woman's tongue, but she nodded. "Thank you. I'll keep it in mind."

Yeah, Dakota just bet she would. Mrs. McDiarmid moved off. A group of singles from Creekside Fellowship descended on the booth like vultures, and Dakota settled into the rhythm of selling.

AT THE END of the day, Travis helped Dakota pack the few remaining goodies into one box then lifted it into her car's hatchback. "Where are these going?"

"Lyssa bought the rest to serve at the Pot of Gold Treasure Hunt's rally later. Don't tell anyone, but I gave her a deal for cleaning us out."

"Makes me wish I'd signed up for that thing."

Dakota laughed. "Like you've got time to traipse up and

down mountain trails looking for geocaches. It'd be quicker to learn to bake."

"Hey, now. Don't think I didn't notice you set aside one of those cakes for Toby."

She shot a quick glance at their son, slumped into a chair, half asleep. "Shh."

"Unless it was for you instead?"

"Of course not!"

Travis grinned. "If it's for Toby, I should take it. He and I can share it tonight for bedtime snack."

"There's like six pieces there! He'd get a tummy ache."

"I don't mind eating most of them. To protect his gut, you understand."

"Right." She ran a hand over Toby's sweaty brow. "You're not bringing him into town for the fireworks tonight?"

"It's a long drive and way past his bedtime."

Dakota nodded, not meeting Travis's gaze.

"Hey. You could come up to the ranch. We've got a few rockets to pop off later."

"Oh, I couldn't…"

Travis glanced around, but no one seemed to be paying them any mind. "I'd like it if you did. So would Toby."

"Is your father going to be there?"

He frowned. "Probably. Why?"

"He doesn't approve of me."

Travis shrugged. "He doesn't approve of anyone. Not me, for sure."

"But you're his firstborn. Of course, he loves you."

"You'd think so, but you'd be wrong. Or, if he does, he's got a strange way of showing it." Travis reached down and hoisted his sleepy boy into his arms. He smoothed Toby's sweaty hair to the side. "When I think of how much I love this kid, I understand my father less than I did before."

Dakota's dark eyes latched onto his, and something passed between them.

"I'd do anything for Toby, Dakota. I hope you know that."

She searched his face. "I do."

"Some of the things I've done have been very hard. Like letting you drive away."

"I don't understand."

"Come up to Rockstead tonight? We can talk."

Dakota rubbed Toby's shoulder. "I'll see. Don't count on it." She gave Travis a quick glance and backed away. "Scotty will be here any minute to load up the shelving unit."

Honestly, there weren't that many people Travis was a fan of, but Dakota's brother was near the bottom of the list. He quirked a grin. "I guess that's my cue to get this little cowpoke out of your way and up to the ranch."

"He's never in my way."

That wasn't what Travis had heard. But at this moment, the rumors of her dating life didn't make sense. And even if she did go out, he believed her. Toby was never an inconvenience.

"Okay. Give me a call." Man, why couldn't he just leave? Dakota was like a magnet, and he was just barely strong enough to resist snapping against her and holding her close. Kissing her, and not a peck on her cheek, either.

Whoa.

He gave her a sharp nod, pivoted on his heel, and strode away.

Those were definitely not thoughts he could act on any time soon. That little smooch he'd dropped on her earlier had been a dumb thing to do. She hadn't asked for it, hadn't welcomed it, though she hadn't slapped him for it, either. It might have gotten in under her skin. Might have done him some good, but he couldn't do it again without the talk they seemed to have promised each other.

He didn't want to do it again, anyway. It had been completely unsatisfying, catching a whiff of perfume and her smooth skin when what he really wanted was a full taste of her.

Travis beeped the truck doors unlocked and lifted Toby into his car seat. "Hey, cowpoke. We're going home now, okay? Do you need Daddy to buckle you in, or can you do it?"

Toby blinked a few times. "I do it."

"Okay."

Wouldn't it be the best thing in his boy's world if he and Dakota got back together? Made it official, this time?

But what if he tried to leap the chasm and fell short? Then things would be a thousand times worse than they'd been. He couldn't risk it. But he also couldn't *not* risk it.

Just a tiny hint of encouragement from her, just a few encounters where they'd managed not to fight, and look at him. A goner in the blink of an eye.

CHAPTER ELEVEN

Dakota was nuts. She knew it, but still her car wound its way up the long, twisty drive to Rockstead Ranch. She was doing this for Toby. He was finally old enough to enjoy fireworks — or so she hoped — and the Fourth fell on a weekend. Why should Travis have all the fun of celebrating that with their son?

And how long had it been since she'd thought of Toby as *their* son, not just hers? Since he was only a few weeks old.

Still, this was probably not the smartest move. All Travis's brothers and stepbrothers and sisters would see them together, and they'd think... what would they think? That she and Travis were back together, which they definitely were not.

She rounded the next curve and pressed her fingertips to her cheek where the light pressure of his lips this afternoon still pulsed. If they weren't together, or something like it, she should have protested that familiarity. But she hadn't. In fact, she'd nearly turned her head just slightly and caught him with her lips.

Such a bad idea.

So was this jaunt, but she drove past the ranch house, down the track to the row of cabins beyond, and parked beside Travis's truck. She was here now. She'd keep her head on her shoulders for Toby's sake, and no one would get hurt.

Toby stood in Travis's open doorway. "Mama! You came."

Dakota swung out of the car and scooped the little boy up. "How could I miss fireworks with my favorite cowboy?"

He frowned and peered into her eyes. "Daddy's a cowboy. I's just a cowpoke."

"He's got you there." Travis leaned in the doorway, a teasing glint in his eyes. He looked far too good in denim shorts, a black T-shirt, and bare feet. No sign of his usual hat, either.

"You don't look much like a cowboy tonight."

Travis reached out and tugged her hat lower on her forehead. "Mama look great, doesn't she, Toby? Tonight, she's a cowgirl."

Their boy looked between them, smiling.

Getting ideas.

Dakota lowered him to the deck floor. "Do you guys still set off the fireworks by the corral?"

Travis's eyes darkened. "Yep."

Was he remembering the same evenings she was? Probably. But then why wasn't he pushing her away? He shouldn't have invited her.

She shouldn't have come. Pretending it was all for Toby had been a mistake. It was maybe twenty percent for her son. The rest was for her, if she were truly honest with herself. She wasn't going to be that honest with anyone else, though. Definitely not Travis.

Toby tugged her toward the cabin door, but it was still full of Travis. Then their son grabbed his daddy by the other hand and grinned between them.

Uh oh. Dakota pulled her hand free. "I shouldn't be here."

A scowl settled on Travis's face. "It's not all about you, Dakota."

"Don't you think I know that? But he's getting ideas, and I hate for him to be crushed."

"Then don't crush him."

What? She stared at her ex, finally realizing her mouth hung open and snapping it shut. "I'm pretty sure you don't realize what you just said."

"I'm pretty sure I do."

But if he did, wouldn't there be some sort of tenderness in his voice, on his face? Because all she saw was the impassive wall he was so good at. A barricade... hiding what, exactly?

She didn't need to waste her time guessing. The guy ran hot and cold. Had forever. Back when she'd liked the hot, it had seemed worth the cold. Until the hot boiled over one too many times.

Sage was right. People didn't really change. Not down deep at the core.

Sure, Travis was trying right now, but how long would it last? How could she trust anything different?

He's got a real relationship with God now. A deeper faith than he ever had back then.

True. But he'd given no evidence of it while they'd remained at odds. He'd been just as rude and prickly as ever.

"Dakota?" His voice softened slightly. "You're already here. Just give us an hour or two."

"There are rules," she blurted out.

Travis's eyebrows shot up. "Aren't there always?" He rubbed Toby's shoulders where their son leaned against him.

Of course, there were. She'd broken her own far too many times. The fact Toby existed was proof of that. But she was stronger now. She didn't care so much about whether Travis's heart would remain intact. That was his problem, and one he would likely navigate just fine. She cared about her own heart, because she knew it wouldn't take much to lose it to this man again. But, mostly, she cared about Toby's.

And God's. She didn't want to grieve her Savior again. That was the bottom line.

Dakota lifted her chin and looked straight at Travis. "I'm here for him."

"I know." He heaved off the doorframe and turned to the interior, guiding Toby with him. "Won't you come in for a few minutes while we get ready?" he tossed over his shoulder.

"I'll wait out here, thanks." She dropped to the top step and leaned her elbows on her knees.

"Suit yourself."

The door closed, and Dakota could hear Toby's high-pitched voice inside, with his dad's lower tones in reply. She shouldn't have come. She should hop in her car and go back to Jewel Lake right now.

Right now.

Except Toby knew she was here.

"Hi, Dakota!" Riley stood nearby, a big smile on her face. "Are you here for the fireworks? I didn't know you were coming."

"I shouldn't be," Dakota blurted out. "It was a bad idea."

"Is it ever a bad idea to make good memories for a little boy?"

"If they turn out to be bad memories because his parents can't stop fighting, yes."

"Then don't fight." Riley held up her hand to stop the barrage she must know was coming next. "Seriously. Whatever happened between you guys was before my time, and you don't owe me an explanation. But why don't the two of you just sit down and talk things through?"

Dakota stared at her friend. "It is definitely not that simple."

"But you really loved each other once. You must have talked about things then." Riley settled on the grass nearby, cross-legged.

"Not really. We fought hard and made up more... ah... physically." Dakota glanced over her shoulder, but the door to the cabin remained tightly closed. Still, she lowered her voice. "Besides, you're hardly one to talk. You and Adam lied to each other for months about how you felt."

Riley pulled a stem of grass and tore it into pieces. "You're right. We had a lot to overcome. We started off on the wrong foot by deciding to pretend to be in love. Then, when the feelings started becoming real, we couldn't trust what we thought we saw in the other person, since we'd done a convincing job of pretending all along."

"Not as convincing as you think."

"Oh?"

"It was the other way around. You thought people were fooled into believing you were in love, when in reality, we could see the truth. That you really did adore each other. You were only fooling yourselves, in the end."

Riley shook her head, grinning. "We did overcomplicate things. But, I think, so are you and Travis."

"I doubt it."

"We pretended to be in love, but you guys are pretending to hate each other."

Dakota clenched her hands together. "We don't hate each other. Exactly."

"I'm glad you see that. Because from where I sit, it looks a lot like dancing around admitting you're in love. Not that different from Adam and me last fall."

"I've noticed before that when people fall in love, they tend to see others through rose-colored glasses." Dakota forced a chill to enter her voice, even though she wanted to believe everything Riley said. "They think everyone is in love and simply needs a little nudge in what they see as the right direction. Believe it or not, that's not always the truth."

"You're right. I'm meddling where I wasn't invited to." Riley got to her feet then looked back at Dakota. "But I happen to believe I'm right, and that you guys are in denial. Think how much Toby's life would improve if you and Travis just talked this thing out?"

Dakota snorted. "Think how much worse Toby's life would be if we gave him hope and then snatched it away, making things far more awkward than before?"

"Or you could try praying about it. Together."

Travis spread out an old blanket on the ground near the corral, ignoring inquisitive looks from his family. But not everyone respected his unspoken keep-away vibes. Not his half-sisters.

The twins sauntered over, a quilt flung over Alexia's shoulder.

"Hey, Toby." Emma crouched to the boy's height. "Want to watch the fireworks with us?"

"He's staying with us," Travis said curtly. "He doesn't really remember them clearly from last year, and I don't want him to be afraid."

Alexia raised her eyebrows. "We won't let him be."

"I said no."

"Loosen *up*, big brother."

"Get lost."

"If he's with us, you guys can smooch with nobody watching," Alexia offered.

A slightly strangled sound may or may not have come from Dakota. Travis wasn't about to check. "There's no smooching. Leave it, Alexia."

She shrugged and flicked the quilt out, not quite touching his. "We'll be right here."

Travis's hands itched to grab that quilt and haul it to the other side of the corral. He'd bodily transfer each twin, as well. But wouldn't that just prove their point? That he wanted to be alone with Dakota? He should have let Toby choose. But, on the other hand, what if Dakota hopped in her car and drove back to Jewel Lake right then?

He was trapped.

He hated being trapped. If anything flared his ire, it was this helpless feeling, knowing she needed to capitulate against his will or make things worse.

Dakota had ambushed him so many times.

As though he hadn't been a grownup who stepped willingly into her snares. Until he'd snapped. Then she had. And it had taken four years for them to speak to each other civilly again. Every one of those two-hundred-ish exchanges of their son in those years had seen one or both of them biting their tongues or wishing they had. Well, him, anyway. He couldn't speak for Dakota.

Except he could, because she'd asked for a truce from their hostilities. She wouldn't have asked if she didn't feel the same.

Travis didn't answer the twins. What was there to say he wouldn't regret later? He was so tired of regrets. Now he dropped to the middle of his blanket, as far from the twins as he could get and still leave room for Dakota.

He gathered Toby into his lap. "Hey, cowpoke. See Uncle Blake over there? He's going to shoot off the fireworks. They'll make a big noise and then fly way up in the sky and make beautiful lights."

"It's called pyrotechnics, Toby." Emma leaned closer. "Pyro means fire."

Travis glared at his sister in the dusky light. "Pretend we're not here."

She shrugged but turned away, flipping her hair over her shoulder.

Out of his periphery, Dakota took a seat on the blanket beside him, leaving a few inches between her shoulder and his.

So, yeah, he'd like to close that gap because he was some sort of glutton for punishment. But not with Toby on his lap and the twins right beside him.

Lord, help me not to screw this up again.

"Three! Two! One!" Blake called out, then lit the fuse.

Boom!

Toby shrieked and jammed his hands over his ears, pressing hard against Travis's chest.

Travis's arms tightened around the boy. "Look. Isn't it pretty?"

Toby whimpered, and Travis pictured his little boy's eyes scrunched tight.

"There's gonna be another one. Look up and see the sparkles."

Boom!

Toby scrambled across the gap to his mama as Dakota reached for him. He straddled her with his legs around her middle and his arms squishing her neck so tightly Travis wondered if she could even breathe. But she bent over him, holding him close and murmuring words Travis couldn't quite make out.

This was not how he'd envisioned the evening. He'd thought Toby would be enthralled, not terrified. Had he done a lousy job of explaining what was going to happen? No. But somehow his little boy hadn't heard his daddy's words.

Boom!

Likely the fireworks were as great as every year. Travis wouldn't know. They were just a series of loud shots and squeals and showering light that scared his kid half to death.

He braced the arm nearest Dakota on the blanket behind them then reached over and rubbed Toby's trembling back with his other hand. "Hey, Toby. You okay?" His fingers bumped into Dakota's, doing the same thing.

She didn't jerk away from his touch, so he didn't, either. In fact, she paused just long enough that Travis covered her hand with his. She still didn't twitch, but Toby relaxed a tiny bit.

That was all Travis needed. He shifted ever so slightly, just enough that his arm touched Dakota's back. She didn't pull away. It might have been his imagination, but it almost seemed like she increased the pressure.

Who needed fireworks in the sky? Sparks were flying right here on the ground.

CHAPTER TWELVE

W hat was she doing?

Dakota hauled her hand out from beneath Travis's and pulled away from the pressure on her back. Suddenly she felt chilled all over, except her front, where Toby was wrapped around her, still wincing. Still shaking. She doubted he'd seen even one of the cascades of light in the sky.

"This isn't working. I'm taking him back to your cabin."

"But—"

It was his weekend. Right. But this was also his family, and there was no way in the world she wanted to sit here and stare at the stupid fireworks amid all these Cavanaghs while Travis and Toby retreated without her.

It was hard to stand up with an octopus strapped to her torso.

Travis stood in front of her and tried to lift Toby away from her, but the kid was having none of that. He wanted his mama. Period. There had been plenty of times where that would have fed Dakota's ego and made her feel superior, but not today. Not when Travis was trying so hard, when he'd truly believed their little boy would love the event.

Dakota reached up and grasped both Travis's hands, allowing him to haul her upright. There was no danger of Toby falling, that was for sure.

"What's up?" Alexia wanted to know.

"He's freaking out," Travis said curtly. "I'm putting him to bed."

"Uh huh." In the flash of light from the next explosion, Dakota could see the skepticism on the teen's face.

And then she realized she was still holding both Travis's hands. She let go, wrapped her arms around Toby, and took a few steps backward, nearly tripping over Noah and Nathaniel. When had they sat down there? She hadn't even noticed. What had they seen? Travis with his arm practically around her?

Great. Good thing they wouldn't be able to see the deep flush she could feel on her face right now. "Sorry. Excuse me."

"No problem." Which of the guys said that, Dakota wasn't certain.

She carried Toby around the horse trailer and down the lane.

Travis reached for the boy, but she turned away. "I've got him."

"He weighs a lot."

"I'm used to it."

"I'm just trying to help."

Dakota took a deep breath. "I know. Sorry."

"It's my fault. I know he doesn't like loud noises."

She'd known that, too. Somehow, she'd thought the flares of light would be compensation enough. They hadn't been. She stumbled on the bottom step — hard to see where she was stepping with her arms full.

But Travis's arm came around her, supporting her and Toby both. He seemed to be offering so much. Why couldn't she just lean into him and believe he'd changed? Maybe he hadn't transformed enough to make things work. Maybe *she* hadn't.

He opened the door and pointed to Toby's bedroom.

She hadn't been back there since their son had been a baby. She'd only been in the cabin at all a handful of times, mostly to exchange insults with Travis.

Dakota had definitely not done her part to mend their relationship. That Travis hadn't, either, didn't count. She was responsible for her own actions and reactions.

She sat on the edge of Toby's bed. "Hey, buddy. Let's get you into pajamas and tuck you in bed. You're safe here in Daddy's cabin."

Was Dakota? Sure didn't feel like it. She pushed the thought aside and took in the bedroom, illuminated only by a nightlight with a bronc silhouetted against the glow. The space was full of denim and red bandana fabric. Shelves lining one wall were loaded with horse and cowboy action figures, making her cringe at the thought of his Toy-Story-themed room in town. It seemed so babyish compared to this.

Then Travis entered the room, seeming to fill every bit of what had been empty space. He crossed to the dresser and pulled out a pair of pajamas.

Dakota had never seen them before. They both kept

clothing at home, sending the boy back and forth wearing whatever he'd come in the week before.

Travis knelt in front of them. "Arms up, buddy."

Toby shuddered a breath and obeyed. Travis tugged the boy's T-shirt up over his head and replaced it with a soft long-sleeved pajama top.

"Now you need to climb off Mama and let's do your bottoms."

"Okay." Toby backed off her and stood. "Need to potty."

Travis nodded, and the boy dashed out.

Somehow that left Travis still kneeling in front of Dakota where she sat on Toby's bed. She couldn't help it, but reached to smooth unruly hair by his ear. "You're so good with him."

"Thanks. That means a lot." Travis's dark eyes met hers. "And you're an awesome mother. Not that there was ever any doubt you would be." He lifted his hand, and his fingers caught hers, ever so gently.

The toilet flushed.

She pulled her hand away as she surged to her feet, nearly toppling Travis to his backside on the plank floor. "I should go now."

"Mama, tuck me night-night?"

"But Daddy…"

"Daddy will go out in the kitchen and put on a pot of coffee so he and Mama can talk." At her muffled protest, Travis held up his hand. "Decaf. Take your time." Then he disappeared.

Dakota gathered her little boy tight. "Let's get you in your jammie bottoms and brush your teeth. Then we'll sing a song and say our prayers, okay?"

"Okay."

A few minutes later she'd tucked him in, singing 'Away in a Manger.' He hadn't let her get away without since last Christmas. Did he make Travis sing it, too? Then Toby murmured thanks for Mama and Daddy and Clover and Alexia and Emma and fell asleep before he'd whispered amen.

Dakota drew the covers to his chin and kissed his soft cheek. "Dear Jesus. I pray You will give Toby sweet dreams and that You will look after him. Thank You. In Jesus' name, amen."

"Amen," came Travis's quiet echo from the doorway as the coffeepot gurgled in the other room.

She should leave now, but she wasn't going to. Not when Travis was acting like a civilized human who actually cared about her and their son. Could she really open her heart and give him a second chance? Not likely... but maybe. She'd hear him out, anyway.

"LET's sit out on the steps." Travis knew staying inside with their chaperone sound asleep would be a lousy idea. Whichever way this thing went between him and Dakota, the temptation would be great. Besides, his brothers' cabins were nearby, and he didn't need to hint at any impropriety. Not now, when they already shared a son, and everything seemed so fragile.

Not looking at him, Dakota poured a coffee. "Good idea."

Maybe she wasn't unaffected by him. Crazy thoughts.

He *knew* she wasn't immune. But was she smart enough to walk away again? Or, more to the point, was she smart enough to give him another try?

Travis breathed a prayer as he filled his own mug and followed her out to the steps. He flipped off the porch light while he was at it. Maybe they'd talk more easily in the darkness.

She sat. So did he, leaving a few inches between them.

Adam and Riley strolled by toward their place, arms around each other, heads bent together. Riley laughed softly.

Something inside of Travis yearned for what his step-brother and his wife shared. He and Dakota had been so close once, but their selfish desires had overruled their common sense. Everything had fallen apart after she became pregnant with Toby then had proceeded from bad to worse until they couldn't be in the same room without yelling at each other or, just as bad, making snide, stabbing comments.

"I'm sorry," he said simply.

Next to him, Dakota shifted slightly. "For?"

"Where do I even start?" Travis chuckled ruefully. "I pushed you into having sex. I didn't see what the big deal was, waiting." His eyes tracked Adam and Riley until they disappeared inside their cabin. "Now I get it. I know I stole something from you that could never be given back. I wish I could do it over again, but I can't."

Dakota cradled her mug in both hands and took a sip. "I could have said no."

"You did."

"Travis, I was a willing participant. We were both wrong."

"And I'm sorry about my temper. I know that was a big part of our problems."

"My dad hit my mom the day before. I... freaked."

He hadn't known that, though he knew they were far from ideal parents. "I would never have hit you."

"Travis, that chair didn't miss my head by much."

He cradled his head in his hands, shame infusing him. "I know. I'm sorry. I really am. God's been working on me about how I handle anger."

"I will forgive you if you forgive me," she said softly.

"There's nothing to forgive." Not compared to how he'd treated her.

Dakota sighed. "If we're going to have a genuine discussion, then we need to be honest. Otherwise, we're just pretending that a little sticky bandage with happy faces on it is going to fix a bone-deep injury."

He hated that she was right. "Okay. You hurt me. You did. And I forgive you."

"I forgive you, too. We were both at fault."

Shouldn't forgiveness feel lighter? It did, a little, but it still seemed something could go wrong at any second. "So, where do we go from here?" He knew where he wanted to go.

"Do we have to go anywhere? Why can't this be enough?"

Travis angled toward her on the step, examining her face in the dim glow of the twins' porch light next door. He should've left his on... except then she could read him easily, too. Here went nothing. "Because I've never stopped caring for you. Loving you. Even when you went out with a dozen other guys—"

Dakota laughed.

He froze. "You asked for honesty. I'm giving it to you." See if he'd go there again, not if she was going to make fun of him.

"You don't get it. I have not been in a dating frenzy."

"You haven't? Everyone sure thinks…"

"What I wanted them to think. I didn't want anyone to feel sorry for me, sitting home and pining away for my baby's daddy."

"I don't understand."

"Sure, I went out a few times — not many — but it was all for show, not because I cared about the guys."

Travis barely dared breath. "Then why the display?"

"Because I knew word would get back to you. I hoped it would."

"Because?"

"I wanted to hurt you."

He swallowed hard, but it didn't soothe the buzzing in his ears. "You succeeded."

Dakota nodded, ever so slightly. "I'm sorry about that."

All those rumors. All those times people gave him pitying looks because his son's mama was busy living it up on weekends when their child was with him at the ranch. It had all been a show? "I don't get it. You didn't care what people thought then, but you do now?"

"I know it doesn't make sense." She hesitated. "To be honest, it was partly in reaction to what I was hearing about you. About your girlfriend in Missoula."

He snorted. "I had no girlfriend in Missoula or

anywhere else. When would I ever have had time? Don't you remember how hard Declan works us here? And with me taking Saturdays off for Toby, trust me, he got the work out of me Monday through Friday."

"The rumors were convincing."

Travis angled a glance at her. "They were."

Blake came up the lane and turned in at his place. He didn't seem to notice them sitting out on the steps. Just as well. Travis wasn't into answering questions. There was still far too much he didn't know. Didn't understand.

"So, where *do* we go from here?" he repeated. "We owe it to Toby to fix things if we can."

"We owe it to Toby not to drag him into something we're not sure we can finish."

"We can decide to finish it."

Dakota shook her head. "Life isn't all mind over matter, Trav. I need to know, deep down inside."

He already did. If Dakota would only accept him back into her life, he'd make sure she didn't regret it. He'd do everything in his power. But what could he do or say to reassure her right now?

Only one thing. He slipped his arm around her waist as he shifted closer. "Trust me?"

Travis waited until she looked up at him. Really looked.

He touched her cheek with his other hand. "I've never stopped loving you, Dakota. I know I've been terrible at showing it, but I want to prove it to you. Now and always." He leaned a little closer, and when she didn't pull away, he pressed his mouth to hers.

After a couple of seconds, she yielded against him. Her

hands came around his shoulders and her lips melded with his.

She tasted of everything good and right in this world. She tasted of hope and trust and, maybe just a little, of Toby's sweaty brow.

"I love you, Dakota," he whispered in the brief instant when he gathered her into a better angle. "I love you so much."

And then she tangled her fingers in his hair and pulled him closer, crushing her mouth to his.

This. This was what he'd been craving for the past four years. Maybe for his whole entire life.

CHAPTER THIRTEEN

Dakota couldn't stop grinning the whole winding way back to Jewel Lake. The little townhouse she shared with Toby wasn't really home. Not like the sheltering she found in Travis's arms.

It seemed too good to be true. Maybe it *wasn't* true. Maybe she'd imagined the whole thing. She'd done pretty well immersing herself in memories after she and Travis split up four years ago, right to the point where it all seemed real until she woke up, crying and alone.

That wouldn't happen again. She was going to do her part to make this become a permanent reality.

She angled her car into her parking spot just as an oncoming vehicle turned into the drive on the other side of the duplex. Sage was arriving. Great timing.

There was nothing Dakota could do to avoid her friend. And Sage *was* her friend. Just because the other woman was lonely and had strong opinions didn't mean Dakota didn't like her. But now wasn't the time.

Except it was. Dakota pushed the car door open and

grabbed her purse, half-hoping Sage would hurry into her side of the duplex. Of course not.

"Hey!" called Sage. "I didn't see you out at the fairgrounds."

"I bet there were hundreds of people there. Maybe even thousands." Dakota went only on past experience here.

"Were you there? Where were you sitting?"

So much for evasion. "No, not tonight."

Sage's eyebrows shot up. "Where were you then?"

Dakota silently counted, but only made it to three before Sage blurted out, "at Rockstead?"

"Yes."

"With Travis?"

Of course, with Travis... and Toby. Could there ever be another reason for braving Declan or all those brothers? Not a chance. Still, she hedged. "For Toby's sake. It was a good thing I was there, too, because the fireworks freaked him out, and we wound up taking him back to Travis's early."

"To Travis's."

"That's what I said."

"You're playing with fire, sweetie."

Didn't she know it? "I think you missed the part about doing it for Toby."

"I don't think I missed anything, Dakota. I'm worried about you. I know you're a little blind where Travis Cavanagh is concerned, but this can't end well."

"He's changed." She had to believe that.

"I'm sure he wants you to think so."

"Sage? You're a Christian. How can you say God can't work in someone's life to effect real change?"

Her friend huffed. "I didn't say that."

"You pretty much did, and you've said it before."

"In theory, it can happen. Only, it rarely does, because people are still humans. Old habits die hard."

"That part is true. But remember that when we come to Jesus, old things pass away, and all things become new."

"I believe the same as you, Dakota. I do. It just so rarely sticks."

"The Apostle Paul, for one." Dakota pressed on. "He went around capturing Christians until he met Jesus for himself. Then he became a brave preacher."

"And that took a supernatural act of God. How many people do you know who've had an experience like Paul's? Zero, that's how many. Not even Travis."

Hard to argue with that, especially as it was nearly midnight and it had been a super long day, starting with the bake sale. Never mind all the emotions on high alert ever since Travis brushed her cheek this afternoon. And then, oh, those kisses this evening. She'd nearly lost herself in them, nearly begged to stay.

So, yeah, she could see what Sage meant. It wouldn't have taken much for Dakota to revert tonight and reject the roads she'd forged in the past four years. It likely wouldn't have taken much for Travis, either, for all his talk. From all she knew, male hormones were pretty focused on just one thing. Sex.

Sure, there'd been tenderness, but there'd also been need. On both their parts. Things hadn't gotten out of hand, but they could have.

Sage was more right than Dakota would like to admit.

Dakota yawned. "It's sure been a busy day, and I'm tired. I hope you had a good day, too?"

"I did. I went to the fireworks with Lyssa and Kirk and Kirk's brother, Dale."

She couldn't resist the impulse to turn the tables on her friend. "Any sparks?"

"Between Dale and me? You're kidding, right? I don't like him even a little bit."

"Because you still love Caleb," Dakota said softly.

"I don't know why everyone thinks that."

"Because it's true?"

Sage huffed. "Not a chance. The guy is so totally full of himself that there isn't room for anyone else in his life."

"But if he changed?"

"And I think we've come full circle. Caleb isn't the changing kind. No more than Travis is."

Dakota shifted in the cooling night air. "How do you pray for people if you don't believe it's even possible for God to answer your prayers?"

"That's not…" Sage's voice drifted off.

"Isn't it? I'd rather believe the best in people. Sure, I know I'll be disappointed sometimes, but at least I'll leave room for God to work. I can have faith. Little changes can give me hope for bigger ones." New thoughts, for sure.

"And when you get crushed, you'll remember you let your emotions get ahead of your logic."

"Logic isn't everything." Hadn't Travis asked her to trust him? That had been a leap if ever there was one after their history. "Hebrews eleven talks about faith being confident of things we can't see. Of believing and trusting when it doesn't look possible. I'm going to live by faith, Sage, and

I'll pray for you, that you'll be willing to take that leap yourself."

"I don't want to jump off a cliff."

"Do you think Paul wanted to get knocked off his donkey by a blinding light and become challenged to turn his life around? Pretty sure the answer is negative. But afterward? Do you think he regretted it later?"

"That's not fair, Dakota. We've already established supernatural intervention in his life."

"We have. It's true. But I believe there's evidence it happens all the time, though perhaps not usually in such dramatic ways. I know I'd like to be open to God's wild and crazy ideas." That had changed since a few weeks back. "Don't you?"

Sage sighed. "Good night, Dakota. Does this mean you're coming to Creekside Fellowship in the morning to sit beside Travis?" There was a hint of sarcasm in her voice.

"No. I'm off to Grace, as usual." Dakota bid her friend a good night and went inside.

There was nothing like a good dose of Sage to dissipate the pleasure she'd felt with Travis and then all the way back to town.

Could Sage be right?

TRAVIS SAT at one end of the tables pulled together at the Golden Grill on Sunday after church. Blake and Ryder sat across from him and Toby, while Adam, Riley, Nathaniel, and Noah filled the other end of the table. Nothing like keeping the Cavanaghs and the Andersons separate, something Travis normally applauded.

Kathryn hadn't come to church today — she missed very rarely — and Declan had picked up the twins right after the service and hauled them back to the ranch, quite against their will. Alexia looked mighty stormy, actually.

Travis thanked God, not for the first time, that Toby was a boy, not a girl. He'd mess up for sure if he had a daughter. Look at Declan. He'd been lousy enough with his sons, but he never said or did anything right with Emma or Alexia.

Toby turned to Travis. "Mama like da fireworks?"

Blake snorted from across the table then tried to cover it up.

"She did." In all the ways. "But you didn't."

Toby pressed his hands to his ears. "Too loud."

"Might want to give him a pair of earmuffs next time," put in Ryder. "There are a few pairs around the ranch."

"Yeah. Never thought of it." Travis wore them himself if he drew the short straw to keep the lawns mowed around the house and cabins. He played with the dark wisps of hair around Toby's neck until the little guy giggled and squirmed. "Sorry, cowpoke. But the sparkles were pretty, right?"

Toby scrunched his eyes. "Too loud."

Blake shook his head. "He didn't even look?"

"Guess not." Travis sighed. "Too busy freaking out."

"At least he had his mama there to comfort him." Ryder's eyes twinkled, and his cheeks twitched.

"Handy, that." Blake exchanged elbow digs with Ryder.

"Yeah, it was nice for him." Travis hated to admit it, but it was still true.

"And for you?"

"Shut it, Ryder."

"Mama says dat's a bad word."

"Mama's right," said Blake solemnly. "Your daddy shouldn't say it."

"Enough out of both of you." Travis glared at his brothers. When was the food ever going to get here, anyway? They'd ordered at least fifteen minutes back.

The server began setting down plates at the Anderson end of the table. Didn't she know to start with the kid? Toby looked longingly at Nathaniel's food.

"Hey, squirt. Want a French fry?"

Toby nodded enthusiastically, and Nat nudged his plate closer for the boy to help himself. A moment later Toby's grilled cheese and tomato soup was set in front of him, then Travis's bacon cheeseburger finally arrived.

"Let's pray," Adam announced.

Everyone, including Toby, ducked their heads while Adam proclaimed gratitude for the food. Then the table got very quiet while the guys and Riley dug into their loaded plates.

"Cavanagh."

Travis looked up to see Dakota's brother, Scotty, staring down at him. "Which one? A whole lotta Cavanaghs here." For once, he'd claim the Andersons as worthy of the surname Declan had legally awarded them.

"More Cavanaghs than Ericksons," Blake added. It almost sounded like a threat.

Scotty glared at Blake before flicking a glance at Toby then settling back to stare at Travis.

Travis tumbled his hands in a rolling motion. "What do you want, Erickson?"

The guy's chin came up. "I want you to leave my sister alone."

"I want you to shut it."

"Mama say…"

"Toby, enough." Travis rose, pushing back his chair, never taking his focus off Scotty. He felt a surge of satisfaction that he had several inches and probably twenty pounds on Dakota's brother. If the guy swung a punch, Travis could take him out. No problem. "How about you mind your own business?"

Scotty took a step closer, shoving his chest against Travis's. "I'm warning you, Cavanagh."

"Duly noted. Would you like to *not* make a scene in front of your nephew?"

"The kid's too little to figure it out."

"You are completely wrong. About that. About everything."

Bump. Scotty's chest rammed into Travis's. His breath stank of alcohol.

Travis's temper ticked up a notch. "You've been drinking." At noon on a Sunday.

"So what if I have?"

Before Travis had managed another breath, he became aware of Blake and Adam flanking him.

"You might want to step outside," Adam said. "You're creating a scene, and I'm pretty sure Estelle has her finger on 9-1-1 to get some police action if you so much as lay a hand on my brother."

Scotty took half a step back before looking around.

Travis didn't dare take the same luxury, because the guy was just belligerent enough to take a swing at him if he got distracted. And Travis would flatten him if he tried.

"Need me to drive you home, Erickson?" asked Adam.

"No!" Scotty reeled around and headed to the exit in more or less a straight line.

Travis looked between Blake and Adam and did his best to swallow his residual anger. "Thanks." He'd come close to losing his temper.

Blake socked him lightly on the shoulder. "Knew you could handle him, but I didn't want my meal interrupted if the table got tipped over. Besides... the kid, you know."

Travis whirled to see Toby focused on dunking his sandwich in his soup. Whew.

Adam nodded. "It's what brothers do."

Travis had hated this guy's guts since before they were teens. He was pretty sure Adam had felt the same, though Adam was far more easygoing than Travis. But this? Proof that Adam had forgiven him. Had really changed since the old days and their teenage rivalries.

He couldn't help himself but pulled Adam into a quick, tight man-hug as the ire ratcheted down. "Thanks, dude."

Adam gave him a punch on the arm, just like Blake had done. "You'd do the same for me." Then he rounded the table and took his seat beside Riley, who tossed a thumbs-up toward Travis.

Travis sat down beside Toby, finally daring to glance

around the diner. Sage's mom, Estelle, pivoted back toward the kitchen now that the door had shut behind Scotty. Most of the other patrons had gone back to their meals, though a couple of men nodded at him when their eyes met.

He ate a couple of French fries while his nerves settled back down. Then he realized that Toby was dunking fries into his tomato soup. He nudged his son lightly. "Hey, you stealing Daddy's fries?"

Toby grinned. "Unca Nat's."

Travis chuckled as the last of the tension drifted from his body. "Good job, cowpoke. Uncle Nat doesn't need them, anyway." And, for once, he didn't resent the fact that Toby thought of Nathaniel as his uncle.

Could this brotherhood thing be taken too far?

He looked around the table. Nah. It was probably about time.

CHAPTER FOURTEEN

Hi, sweetie."

Dakota looked up from where she was arranging a new shipment of sleeveless western-themed shirts to see her mother coming in the store's front door. "Hi, Mom."

"How are you? I missed seeing you at the fireworks the other night."

Was she going to have to explain herself over and over? Wasn't twenty-seven old enough to make her own decisions without being questioned by everyone and their dog? In her dreams.

"I didn't feel like hanging around at the fairgrounds when Toby was with his dad."

"It's hard for you, sharing your son with that no-account cowboy."

Dakota sighed. "Travis is the son of the most successful rancher in the area. He's hardly no-account."

"He never stepped up to do what was right."

"I don't know how you can say that. We share custody. He pays for all the extras for Toby, like daycare."

Mom leaned in. "He didn't marry you."

"Do you have any idea how old-fashioned it is to get married just because a woman becomes pregnant? It's a lousy reason. A marriage needs more of a foundation than that."

"It worked on your father."

Dakota blinked. "You got pregnant with Scotty so Dad would commit?" Of course, the wedding date and her brother's birthdate clearly proved that her parents had been sexually active before marriage, but...?

Her mother shrugged. "Not completely."

"And you've never regretted that?"

"It's not been all bad, Dakota."

"I don't want the kind of marriage where that's the best that can be said for it."

"You don't act like you want a marriage at all. Going out with different men all the time when Travis has Toby. Can't you settle down to one?"

That's what she intended. Just one. "I will, when the time is right. Someday, I expect to marry a wonderful man who'll treat Toby like his own." Because he would be. Please, Lord.

"I don't think—"

The chime above the door jangled — whew — and a young man of about thirty entered. Dakota did a double-take. Wasn't this the youth pastor over at Creekside? The guy who'd masterminded the Pot of Gold Treasure Hunt?

She took a few steps closer. "Hi. Is there anything I can help you find today?"

"I'm looking for a couple of shirts, actually. Got any casual button-ups, or are they all full-on westerns?"

"Now there's a good-looking guy, Dakota," Mom whispered. "No wedding ring."

By the look of the sudden pink tinge on the tips of his ears, Mom hadn't been quite as quiet as she'd thought. Or maybe Mom wasn't trying to be subtle.

Dakota walked over to the rack on the other side. "These might be more what you're looking for then." She slid a few hangers and pulled out an oatmeal-colored buttoned shirt in a style similar to what he was currently wearing. "Something like this?"

"Possibly." He grinned and came over. "I know we're in the middle of ranch country, but it's not actually my personal style. Kirk Kennedy mentioned you had a wider range of men's shirts here than I expected from the store name."

"Ah, Kirk is married to a friend of mine. Lyssa lived next door to me, with Sage Mulligan."

"Gotcha. I'm Eli Bryson, youth pastor at Creekside Fellowship."

She extended her hand to meet his. "Dakota Erickson. I've heard all about your geocaching challenge. A lot of folks from Grace are participating as well."

"It's not too late to join in." He flashed her a grin. "Although you'd be starting at a disadvantage, since we're already a quarter of the way into this summer's hunt."

"No, that's okay. I work full-time here, and I also have a young son. I don't have much free time."

She heard a mutter from Mom. She probably figured

Dakota was purposefully scaring off a cute guy who might be interested.

"I hear kids can keep their parents on their toes. I have yet to experience that for myself." Eli plucked a hanger off the rack and held up the shirt. "I like this style. Any other colors?"

"Blue, green, and deep red." Dakota knew better than to use the word burgundy on a man. "What size are we looking for? Medium?"

He nodded. "I'll take one in green."

"We have a changing room, so you can try it on."

"It'll fit. I always wear medium."

Men. "We have a great return policy."

Eli grinned again. "Good to know." He took the shirt she extended and walked toward the cash desk, pausing to riffle through a rack of jeans.

Dakota rang up the sale and watched him leave the store.

"Well, you could have handled that better." Mom crossed her arms.

"Oh?"

"You go out all the time. Do you tell every man about Toby up front? Seems like that would turn them off before things ever got started."

"I have never dated a guy who didn't know about Toby."

"No wonder you're still single."

"What, I'm supposed to spring his existence later? That hardly seems fair. We're a package deal, my son and me." She could only think of one man to whom that might be considered a bonus, and that was Travis Cavanagh.

Dakota was definitely not ready to discuss that with her mother.

"I WANT the two of you to head into the north ranges for a few days and see how the cows are doing. Check out the grass and decide when we should move them further east." Declan stood in front of the corral gate, legs braced and arms folded across his chest.

Travis gave a sideways look at Adam. "Send me with one of my brothers, not with him."

"Learn to get along."

"It's not that."

Declan's eyebrows shot up.

"Adam's a newlywed. It's not fair to make him go."

His father uttered a bark of laughter. "Nice try." He toggled his finger between them. "I want you out of here first thing in the morning, and don't come back until you've done a headcount."

It was Tuesday evening. This meant no fairgrounds for Toby or for the twins, since no one else was likely to drive the girls down. "We'll be back sometime Friday afternoon."

"If you have the information I need."

Travis stared at his father. "I'm not missing five minutes with my son."

"Make sure you're not shirking."

"Or you could send Blake and Ryder into the backcountry. Then the twins won't miss practice."

Declan waved his hand dismissively. "They don't need

to go. Whenever they spend time in Jewel Lake, they get big ideas from the town kids."

If Travis had felt stifled as a kid, how did the girls feel? All the brothers chipped in some with their sisters, but they weren't any sort of replacement for a loving, hands-on dad. The kind Travis was determined to be.

Adam shoved Travis lightly with his shoulder. "It's okay, dude. I can hack a night or two sleeping on the hard ground without my wife. I'm not as soft as you."

Travis shoved back. "Who're you calling soft?"

Declan snorted and strode away.

Travis and Adam watched him go then turned to look at each other. "What's all that about?" asked Adam. "Is this typical?"

Travis scratched the back of his neck. "Not really. I mean, yeah, I've done it before. You weren't here. Too busy off being a rodeo star."

Adam grinned.

"But do we do this every year in July? Nope."

"So he wants rid of us both for a few days."

Travis laughed. "Probably told the truth. Wants us to learn to get along."

"It's been going better, huh?"

"Yeah. I only hate you a little bit these days."

"Sounds like an improvement."

"Dude. You have no idea."

"I might." Adam searched his face. "You can spill your guts to me on the trail. Should be fun."

"As if." Travis shoved at Adam's shoulder again, just for good measure. "Hey, question for you."

"Hmm?"

"I know you asked Declan for Running Creek Ranch for you and Noah and Nathaniel. He said yes, but…"

"But then he found out I was lying about being engaged to Riley, and he retracted his offer."

"Anything new on that front?"

Adam shook his head. "I don't know how much to push him. I talked to my mom about it a couple of weeks ago."

"What did she have to say?"

"Said to be patient. Seems like I've been doing that forever. Riley and I want to start a family, but we don't really want to keep living in the little cabin when we have a baby, you know?"

"I know."

Adam gave his head a quick shake then glanced around. He lowered his voice further. "Of course, you know. Sorry. It just doesn't seem like any way to live as a family, sitting here under my stepfather's thumb. Riley wants a real kitchen. Our own home. So do I."

"I get it, man. I do." Travis hadn't really thought about it five years ago when Dakota got pregnant. He'd just assumed she'd move into his cabin more permanently and give up her place in town. What had he been thinking?

He hadn't been. Not about that. Not about anything.

At least Adam and Riley would likely have the option of moving into the ranch house next door at Running Creek. It wasn't as big or fancy as the Rockstead house, but who needed eight bedrooms and five bathrooms? Even a blended family of eight kids could barely fill it. Travis didn't know about Adam, but *he* certainly wasn't planning on having eight.

How many would Dakota like? Even one more would

crowd the little log cabin. And Adam was right about the kitchen. No new bride or young mother would want to traipse over to her in-laws' dining room three times a day.

He was getting ahead of himself.

But maybe he needed answers to some of these questions before he and Dakota got in any deeper. He'd already found out once that love could only take them so far. At twenty-three, none of that had mattered.

Five years later, he could see that it did. Even though Dakota hadn't thrown all that at him back then, she should have.

Time to man up, Cavanagh. Get your ducks in a row.

Maybe it wouldn't be so bad to spend a few days with his stepbrother far from any judgmental listening ears. He and Adam could hash out a plan of action for both of them.

And he'd definitely be back for Friday afternoon when Dakota arrived at the ranch with their son.

Maybe he could convince her to stay for a few hours. Get Cook to pack up a picnic on the quiet, maybe. Give him a chance to spend some time with his little family and make sure he wasn't imagining things.

Those kisses on the Fourth of July?

He had definitely not imagined those. He could still smell her light floral scent. Could still feel the imprint of her lips on his.

Life was good.

It was only going to get better.

CHAPTER FIFTEEN

Dakota? I've been looking over the sales reports for second quarter, and they're eighteen percent lower than last year. Can you explain why?"

She froze with her phone to her ear just as she was locking up the store. The daycare closed in seven minutes, and Mrs. Dillonworth complained she were tired of Dakota being the last parent to pick up her child. "This is a bad time, Pete."

"It's always a bad time for you."

"Why not stop by the store tomorrow, and we can talk between customers?" She double-checked the lock and walked toward her car.

"I'm in Oregon."

Of course, he was. "Next time you're in Jewel Lake, then."

"I'm not sure when that will be. Just give me the short version."

"I need to pick up Toby."

"Do you need this job?"

She narrowed her glare on the back of the store. "Of course."

"Then give me five minutes of your ever-so-precious time."

It wouldn't be five. It would easily be thirty or more. "I'll call you back in a few minutes. Say, in about half an hour?"

Pete sighed into the phone. "I don't think you understand."

Wasn't that the pot calling the kettle black? Her temper flared. Next job she took, she'd look for a female boss. Someone with a family. Someone who'd actually realize that kids needed to be picked up from daycare on time.

Maybe it was time for that next job. Like, this week. Only... where? Who was hiring? She'd been here for so long. Too long, obviously.

"Pete, I absolutely cannot talk right now. You called on my personal time. I'm willing to give you part of my evening, but not the next half hour." She tapped her phone to end the call, her hands shaking. Her whole body trembling.

Was she going to get fired over this? Probably. Her boss had been getting more and more unreasonable over the past year. He was rarely in town and never seemed to remember the time difference between Montana and wherever he was.

He was just like Dakota's father.

She paused as she reached for the car door. Really? Pete was just like Dad? Wow, that was true in so many ways. About the same age. Both full of themselves. Both expecting to be in charge every minute. Both happy to let the little woman handle whatever fit within her pea-sized brain's capability.

Maybe she'd subconsciously figured a lifetime of dealing with her dad, one way or another, equipped her to handle Pete. Nothing had been further from the truth.

Enough. This wasn't getting Toby picked up on time. She glanced at the car clock as she shifted into reverse. *Nothing* was getting Toby picked up on time, since she was already late. Great.

"There you are!" The daycare administrator, car keys in hand, stood on the doorstep with Toby. "You've been late a lot recently. Is everything okay?" She guided Toby toward the car as she spoke.

"Hi, buddy." Dakota bent and picked up her little boy, who buried his face in her neck. "I'm sorry, Mrs. Dillonworth. My boss called just as I was leaving the store."

"There's always something, isn't there?"

Dakota's temper flared. "Yes, there always is. I'm sorry. I'm doing the best I can."

The older woman pursed her lips and shook her head. "I cannot ask my staff members to stay past six o'clock for you day after day."

Deep in her purse, her cell rang. Probably Pete again. "I understand, Mrs. Dillonworth."

"Do you? I'm sorry, Dakota. It isn't all about you. Other people have commitments as well."

What exactly was the older woman saying? She wasn't kicking Toby out of daycare, was she? It was six weeks until preschool began over at Creekside Academy, but that was only mornings. Dakota would still need daycare in the afternoons. There was only so much she could accomplish by herself.

Travis had it good. He got to have Toby only on his days off. The two of them could hang out together the whole time. Ride horseback. Play with that toy horse collection. Travis didn't even have to cook meals or figure out snacks.

Dakota had to juggle everything. Every day. She worked six days a week because she needed the money. Only Sundays were off, and she went to church in the morning, to the supermarket after lunch, and by then Travis was there to drop Toby off and the whole week cycled around again. It never ended.

It would be even worse if she lost her job. Or lost the daycare space, which amounted to the same thing, since she couldn't take Toby to work with her.

She stared at Mrs. Dillonworth, feeling her shoulders slump, feeling the tears sting her eyes. She would not cry in front of this woman any more than she'd cry in front of Pete. Or Dad. She would not. "Good night, Mrs. Dillonworth. See you in the morning."

Dakota pivoted back to the car, opened the back door, and swung Toby inside, where he tugged his backpack off before she buckled him in.

"Okay, Mama?" He patted her cheek.

"I will be, baby." She pressed a kiss to his forehead and shut the door.

"Dakota…"

What, the woman still hovered? Dakota hunted for a smile but couldn't find one. "Yes?"

"I wish you all the best."

"And by that you mean?"

"You need to find different childcare by Monday. This just isn't working. We have families on the wait list who will be more dependable."

Dakota opened her mouth and closed it again. She gave a curt nod and rounded the car. She absolutely couldn't think of a single thing to say that she wouldn't have to apologize for later. The words churning around in her head were not ones she wanted Toby to hear, and especially not from his mama.

She drove toward the condo. Should she call Pete back or let him call her again? Which way did she stand the best chance of keeping her job? The one she'd have trouble doing until she could find care for Toby.

Oh, God, why is everything such a mess all of a sudden? But it wasn't sudden. It had been building for a while with her boss. With the daycare.

She could ask Mom to watch Toby, but Mom wasn't dependable. Besides, that would put the little boy in Dad's sphere. And Scotty's. They weren't the kind of role models she wanted for her son.

And the Cavanagh men were?

Not Declan. Maybe Travis's brothers were all right. But that wasn't an option. She wasn't giving Toby up to his daddy, and Travis couldn't do his job with a child underfoot any more than Dakota could. If only she'd stayed at the ranch four years ago, none of this would have happened.

But Travis had been in a bad place back then. His temper... she didn't even want to remember. Besides, neither of them had been living out their faith. They'd needed to break from each other.

How about now?

Dakota flicked on her signal light at her house. She'd better not grab takeout when she wasn't sure her income would hold, even though she absolutely did not feel like cooking. She'd like to drown in chocolate, but Toby needed a real meal with vegetables and protein and all the good stuff that kept a little boy healthy and growing.

She'd put her kid first, as usual. After setting the brake, she rounded the car to let Toby out.

"Okay, Mama?" He looked at her from worried brown eyes.

Dakota hated she'd done that to him. Why couldn't she shelter him and give him everything he deserved? Her mess wasn't his fault.

SHE HADN'T PICKED UP. Did that mean she didn't want to talk to him anymore, after all?

Travis turned his phone over and over in his hands. He needed to get back to his cabin and figure out what he was taking on the trail ride, and the cell signal didn't bounce around the bend.

Try once more.

He pressed Dakota's icon and listened to it ring three times then go to voicemail. He didn't want to leave a message, but she wasn't giving him many options. *Keep it short. Keep it apologetic. Just get the words out.* Finished, he turned off the phone and stuffed it in his hip pocket.

Why hadn't she picked up? It was after work. She and Toby should have been home by now. Maybe she'd stopped at the Golden Grill for supper, and it was too loud to hear her phone ring. Maybe she was out with some other guy and didn't want to talk to Travis. But she wouldn't have kissed him like she had Saturday night if she were seeing someone else, would she? Besides, she'd said there was no one. She wouldn't lie.

Would she?

No. He was letting his old insecurities call the shots in his head again. He'd done what he could, leaving that message, and he'd come back over toward the house later and see if she'd responded. Meanwhile, he needed to pack and coordinate stuff with Adam. Not that he cared about a change of clothes, but a bedroll and enough food were a high priority. Cook was on that part.

"Got what you need?" Adam asked when Travis came back down the lane to the cabins.

"Other than I can't get through to Dakota. I hate leaving a message."

"We should be back in enough time on Friday no problem."

"I've been taking the twins down to the fairgrounds Wednesdays, and picking Toby up from daycare."

"Oh, right. I'd forgotten about that."

Travis hadn't. If he said he was going to do something, he did it. That his father could overrule his time with Toby on a whim irritated the snot out of him. Sure, it wasn't on the weekend, but Declan had allowed the Wednesday excursions until now.

"So, I've got my sleeping bag and a change of clothes." Adam fell into step beside him. "I've got some jerky and protein bars. What kind of stuff is Cook sending?"

"Coffee, salt, and a billycan. What else do we need?"

His stepbrother laughed. "A few cans of chili?"

"Something like that." Still bugged Travis that Dakota hadn't answered. It was going to be a long three days, not knowing what was going on. Not being sure she'd received his message.

"Taking your rifle?"

"What kind of question is that? Always. You never know what you'll run into out there. Wolves. Bears. Mountain lions. I'd like to keep my skin on my body, thanks."

"Just checking."

"You got soft all those years playing rodeo games while the real cowboys did the actual work."

Adam searched his eyes. "I never know whether that's a real dig, or if you're teasing anymore."

"I don't know, either."

"I'm thankful to wonder. Once I knew you'd as soon bump me off a cliff as look at me."

"Maybe it's still that way."

"Dude, what's going on? You're ornery as a dog in a wasps' nest."

"Told you. I can't get a hold of Dakota."

"Bugging you that much? Why not drive down to town?"

"There's too much to do before heading out in the morning. First light is mighty early this time of year."

"Sounds like you're some kind of wuss who needs sleep or something."

"What if I am?"

"You've got it bad, man. Here for years you've been all

about keeping everything separate from her. Lately, I think you've gone and fallen for her all over again."

"I wasn't keeping separate. Not with Toby."

"You snarled at Dakota every chance you got."

"Did not."

"Did, too. Like a coyote caught in a leg trap, not letting anyone in to see if they could help you. Positive everyone was out to cause even more pain."

"They mostly were."

"You listening to yourself?"

Travis huffed a sigh. "Leave it. You asked why I was ornery. I told you. Don't try to make a federal case out of it."

"Sorry, man. Just want you to know Riley and I are praying for you. All of you."

"Thanks." He rubbed the back of his neck. "I'm heading back there to try her cell again. I don't know what's going on, but it's not like her to not pick up. Even when she hated me."

Adam elbowed him. "She doesn't hate you anymore? You guys looked cozy Saturday."

"Yeah, well, status undetermined. But there might be hope." Travis fingered his phone. "Not sure."

"Grab whatever Cook has put together while you're down that way. I'm gonna dig around in the storeroom for some camping supplies."

"A princess like you needs a mattress pad?"

"Nah, it's for *your* tender backside." Adam shoved his shoulder. "Go find out what's happening."

CHAPTER SIXTEEN

"Please eat, buddy."

Toby had already eaten the chopped-up hot dog Dakota had put in the mac'n'cheese. Protein, right? Now he picked out the peas and placed them in a row around the edge of his plate while the sauce congealed. "Is yucky."

"But you always like it." She'd eaten just enough of the lackluster meal to take the edge off her hunger. Toby's assessment was spot on. Was it possible for the powdered packets to go stale?

He hunched a small shoulder. "I he'p Cook make sauce with cheese."

Of course. Anything Dakota could do, the crew at Rockstead could do ten times better. "Well, this is what's for dinner." No informing him she was planning on indulging in some chocolate therapy once she'd tucked him in bed.

She hadn't called Pete back yet. She just couldn't deal with him in front of Toby. Her boss had left a message.

She'd heard the beep, but hadn't looked at her phone. It likely didn't matter whether she'd picked up immediately or called him in two hours. Either way, she was going to be sacked. She'd put off the moment of actuality a bit longer, thanks.

"Toby, eat." Dakota heard the impatience in her voice. Why did he have to pick today of all days to stage a protest?

His lower lip trembled, and he managed to ooze out a crocodile tear. It dribbled down his cheek and plopped on top of a pea.

Patience, Lord. Please. Now.

"Here, let Mama feed you." She reached around and picked up his fork. "You need something in your tummy."

Toby pursed his lips together and turned away, reminding Dakota of his one-year-old self.

"Okay, have it your way. Go get your jammies on. It's bedtime then."

"Is not bedtime!"

"It's either suppertime or bedtime. You pick."

"I want Daddy."

That made two of them. She'd like nothing more than to let Travis deal with his stubborn child tonight. "You can't have Daddy until tomorrow when he brings Clover to the fairgrounds, and Alexia and Emma and their horses, too." Sudden inspiration struck her. "Do I need to call Daddy and tell him you can't go riding tomorrow because you weren't a good boy for Mama?"

Toby scowled at her, picked up a pea from the edge of his plate, and shoved it in his mouth. Then a second one.

Well, it was nice to know there was a threat that

worked. Dakota set the fork within his reach and rose to tidy the kitchen. Where was she going to find a new job? Oh, and a new daycare. And maybe some painkillers to relieve the tension clamping around her head. Ugh.

She washed the pot and her plate and Toby's lunch containers while he slowly stabbed his food, one noodle at a time, sighing heavily between each bite.

I feel you, kid.

Dakota swept the kitchen floor.

Toby still had maybe ten bites left. He could stretch that for five minutes or more.

She grabbed her phone and sat at the end of the table. On the lock screen, she could see her missed call had Travis's name attached, not Pete's. Travis never called, but they were in a new place now, right? How had he known she needed to hear his voice? Why hadn't she at least checked to see who called earlier? She'd been so sure it was Pete.

Pete. Oh, man. Either way, she'd totally blown him off. If he hadn't intended to fire her an hour ago, he most assuredly did now. She leaned her elbows on the table and massaged her temples.

"Mama 'kay?"

Dakota angled a look at her little boy, who wore a worried look on his face, but she couldn't dump all this on a four-year-old. "Finish up your macaroni, all right?"

He stabbed all the remaining noodles with his fork and shoved the whole wad in his mouth, barely able to chew or swallow.

At least he was done. She wasn't going to quibble over the lone pea drowning in the excess cheese sauce. "Good job, buddy." She picked up his plate, washed it, and set it in the drain rack before wiping the table. "Go wash your face."

He scrambled down and was back in a minute. "No tell Daddy."

Daddy. Travis had called. Dakota managed a smile for her son, tapped to listen to the voicemail, and tucked the phone against her ear. She didn't want Toby to overhear in case there were endearments he didn't need to know about.

Dakota, I'm so sorry, but I have to cancel tomorrow. I know Toby's expecting me, but Declan is sending Adam and me into the north range for a few days, and I can't get out of it. He refuses to send one of my brothers. He doesn't much care that he's disappointing Toby and the twins. All he cares about is getting his way.

Dakota heard the frustration in Travis's voice as her gut chilled and tightened. No stinkin' way. And here she'd just used this as a threat. How was Toby ever going to trust her again?

Wait. She'd tuned out the rest of Travis's words. She tapped to listen again.

We're definitely planning to be back Friday by suppertime, but I won't be able to let you know if we're late. I'm sorry. I hate doing this to you. And I know Toby will be upset.

He had no idea.

The odds of catching him within cell range were slim, but Dakota had to try. She tapped his icon, and it went straight to voicemail. Why couldn't Declan invest in some infrastructure and get a signal booster up there? Jeepers, the man was so annoying. So irritating. So cheap.

"Hey there." She eyed Toby, who watched her expectantly. "Thanks for letting me know. I'll handle it from here." Like she always did. "See you in a few days."

Did she have to tell Toby tonight? No. He'd be sure she'd broken her promise. He'd have a conniption fit and refuse to sleep. She'd tell him in the morning before she dropped him off at daycare.

At least he could attend the rest of this week. Whether Dakota had a job tomorrow or not, she'd find out after the little guy was in bed.

Chocolate might not be enough.

Travis saddled Lancaster half an hour before dawn. Where the blazes was Adam? Still snuggled up with his wife while Travis did all the last-minute prep? He'd have to rethink getting along with his annoying stepbrother.

Everything was aggravating or worse. He'd picked up a voicemail from Dakota while he was in the house getting the saddlebags of food Cook had prepared. Dakota's reply had been no message at all. It had been as impersonal as if she were talking to her boss or some complete stranger. What was he supposed to make of that? He had three days to stew about it. Great.

A small sound down the alley in the stable caught his attention. Adam. Finally. But it wasn't. Riley stood in the aisle, looking washed out in a pair of jeans and a T-shirt. "Adam's sick. He's got a fever and a sharp pain in his side. I think I need to take him to the ER. What if it's his appendix?"

"He's not faking it to get out of the trail ride?"

Riley scowled at him. "Of course not. Why would he do that?"

"I know he didn't want to go."

"Well, that doesn't mean he'd rather be in this much pain. Where's your father?"

"Declan?" Travis rejected the familial term. "He'll be out here shortly, I imagine. He wouldn't trust us enough to make sure we left on time without a grand sendoff and a repeat of all the instructions."

"I heard that." Declan came down the dim alley from the other direction then stopped and crossed his arms. "And this is why I can't trust you boys to simply do your work." He turned his glare on Riley. "I'm with Travis. Are you sure he's actually sick?"

Her eyes blazed. "I can't believe you unfeeling bunch. Adam isn't going on this trail ride. I'm driving him to the hospital in Missoula. I'll let you know what the doctors say. As if you care."

"I do." The words erupted from Travis's mouth. "Sorry. Take care of him."

Riley narrowed her eyes at him before offering a sharp nod. Then she turned on her heel and jogged away.

"You believe her, huh?" Declan watched her go.

"Yeah, I do. Adam might not have wanted to do this anymore than I did, but he wouldn't pull a stunt like that. If she says he has a fever and pain, then he does."

"Thought you didn't like him."

Travis shrugged. "I'm getting over it."

"Good. Then you can start on Nathaniel."

"Nath…?"

"Go get him. He's riding out with you. It'll be full daylight soon, and you guys should be on the trail by then."

"But…"

Declan's eyebrows shot up.

"Yes, sir." Travis looped Lancaster's reins over the gate and strode out of the stable. Someone needed to take his father down a peg or two, but it wasn't going to be him. Not today, anyway.

He pounded on Nathaniel's cabin door. "Yo, dude! Get your butt out of bed!"

The door opened and a fully clothed cowboy stared back at him. "Good morning to you, too. What's got stuck in your craw?"

"Adam's sick."

"And?"

"And Declan says you're accompanying me to the north ranges for the next three days instead. We, uh, leave in about fifteen minutes. Everything is packed except your tighty-whiteys."

"Ha-ha." Nathaniel stared at him for a few seconds. "Uh… you're not kidding, are you?"

"Nope. Wish I was." In more ways than one.

Nathaniel drove his hands through his unruly hair. "That son of a gun."

Travis could add a few choice words to that.

"So, this is my official summons, huh?"

"You could say so." At least Travis'd had overnight to get his brain switched over. "What do you need to do? Fill your thermos with coffee? Brush your pearly whites?"

"What, you don't want garlic breath for the next three days? Guess I can brush a time or two if it'll make you feel better. Because Cook had better have sent some good grub along."

"Enough we've got a packhorse for that and the gear."

"Perfect. I'll be down to the stable in a few minutes."

"Want me to saddle Kingpin for you?"

Nathaniel's eyebrows shot up. "You'd do that for me?"

"Sure. Why not? I'm not such a terrible guy, you know."

"Could've fooled me." Nathaniel held up both hands. "Sorry. But you've been pretty stuck-up for, well, forever."

"Yeah, sorry. See you in a few." Travis strode back to the stable without a backward glance. He could imagine Nathaniel's face well enough.

Adam's truck, with Riley at the wheel, roared by in a cloud of dust.

"Time's a wasting." Declan looked up from adjusting the load on the packhorse. "Do I have to do everything for you?"

Do not engage.

Easier said than done. Travis gave his father as wide a berth as possible, grabbed apple slices, and entered Kingpin's box stall. "Hi, there, boy," he crooned, holding out the treat. "Your cowboy will be here in just a minute. How do you feel about letting me saddle you?"

Declan snorted. "Like he's gonna answer you."

"He's answering with his ears." The gelding lipped the chunks off Travis's open palm. Travis ran his hands over the horse before reaching for the bridle. "Here we go."

His father stood in the doorway, feet braced and arms crossed. "That lazy cowboy still in bed when it's nearly daybreak?"

Travis kept his voice steady. "Nope. He was up and

dressed. He's just grabbing a few things and will be here in a minute." He fastened the buckles, reached for the worn saddle, and swung it over Kingpin's back.

The gelding shifted a few steps sideways, but no more than Travis had expected. "Easy, boy." He patted the horse's shoulder. "Cinch time, okay?"

"Thanks, Travis." Nathaniel shouldered past Declan. "I've got it from here."

Kingpin offered a soft whinny and nuzzled his rider.

Travis turned and looked at his father. "Anything else we need to know? I've got the satellite phone, so if you need us, you can find us." He strapped his rifle case to the saddle.

"You're good to go."

"Excellent." Travis walked Lancaster out to the corral where the packhorse waited patiently. He took the lead rope and mounted his horse just as Nathaniel and Kingpin appeared.

Nathaniel gave him a sharp nod, and they headed out past the cabins.

"Nice day for a ride," Nathaniel offered.

Travis relaxed a little. This particular stepbrother of his was pretty easygoing. He could think of worse people to spend three days with. His mind slid to Dakota. Although he'd prefer her company to Nat's.

"Ever regret intimacy with Dakota way back when?"

Nathaniel's tone was mild, but Travis's back turned ramrod straight instantly. So much for easygoing.

CHAPTER SEVENTEEN

"This is your business how?" Travis tugged his hat lower on his brow and glanced at Nathaniel, riding beside him.

"Did you tell yourself it was okay because you were going to marry her anyway?"

"We talked about it and decided we weren't ready for that level of commitment. We were just kids."

"How old were you? Twenty-two? Twenty-three?"

"When we started sleeping together? Dude, this is none of your business. Can we go back to talking about the weather or something?"

Something passed over Nathaniel's face too quickly for Travis to catch it and catalog it.

"I've been wanting to talk to you for a long time."

"To rub in some guilt? Because while the circumstances were far from ideal, I don't regret Toby for one red hot second. That kid is life."

"Take your chip out of your shoulder. Seriously. That's not what this is about."

"Then what?" But he couldn't quite swallow the bite in his voice.

"Me."

"You?" Travis stared at Nathaniel's profile. "What on earth are you talking about?"

"Did you ever meet Ainsley Johnson?"

"Ain — dude, spit it out already."

"We were dating last spring. She's amazing, Travis. I was head over heels."

"Where'd you meet? I don't remember her."

"I sure didn't want to bring her around Rockstead. I guess I thought she might fall for one of my brothers instead. All you guys are so much more macho than me."

Travis snorted.

Nathaniel shrugged. "Just saying."

"You didn't tell me where you met." Or why it mattered.

"She worked in the office at Creekside Academy. I met her once when Eli was in a meeting. I was waiting for him, and Mrs. McDiarmid asked me to run some papers over to the school."

Travis eyed his stepbrother. Nathaniel had actually braved up and asked the girl out?

"She has a great sense of humor, and she's pretty."

Of course, she was pretty. Why didn't the guy get on with the story?

"One thing led to another, and, well, we, uh…"

"Got down to hot-and-heavy business. Understood."

"Yeah. And then she ghosted me."

Not what Travis expected to hear. He blinked. "Ghosted?"

"I never heard from her again. I'd bought a ring already,

because I couldn't imagine life without her. But I guess she felt differently."

"Oh, man. I'm sorry. Sounds rough."

"I don't know what I did wrong. Besides the obvious, but couldn't we have talked about that?"

The poor guy couldn't even say the word *sex* to his brother, and he thought he'd have a heart-to-heart with the girl of his dreams? At least now it made a little sense why he wanted to talk to Travis. Adam had also slept around some in his rodeo years, but never with a woman he cared that much about. Didn't make it better. It just was.

"How do you get over something like that?"

"I don't know. Because Dakota got pregnant, we were forced to stick together to at least some degree."

"I always admired you for that."

Travis frowned. "For what?"

"Owning up. Not abandoning her."

"There's no way I'd do that. My mother walked away from three little boys without a backward glance. I have no idea how she could live with herself all these years. I know what it's like to be missing a parent, and there was no stinking way I was doing that to any kid of mine."

"That's what I mean. You never questioned it. You just did it."

"Didn't make it easy."

"No. I get that."

"Dakota and I fought every single time we came within ten feet of each other. We couldn't seem to help antagonizing each other."

"But that's changed?"

"Yeah. She ended it. Said we needed to call a truce for

Toby's sake. We'd mostly stayed semi-civil when he was around, but… he's noticing more now." Travis shrugged. "It was probably affecting him anyway, and I just didn't notice."

"But now? She was here for the fireworks…"

"Yeah. And those freaked Toby out, so we took him back over to the cabin. Further from the noise."

"That the only reason?"

"What're you getting at?"

"Are you back together?"

Travis wanted to confirm that, but she hadn't picked up his call, and her return voicemail had been just plain formal and weird. "I think so? Maybe? It's gonna take some work."

The horses plodded along the dirt road between the hayfields. They had a long way to go yet today. Nathaniel had been right. It was a nice day for a ride, and he didn't need to push the guy into talking more. They had three days to finish the conversation. Or not finish it. Travis didn't much care, either way.

"It's not only that she ghosted me," Nathaniel said maybe twenty minutes later. "She completely disappeared. No one has seen her since."

Travis swiveled in his saddle to study his stepbrother's face. "That's weird."

"Yeah. You hear about trafficking and stuff, but I don't think that's what happened."

His gut went sick. "How would you know?"

"She moved out of her place. Quit her job. Closed her social media accounts. I talked to the police, and they didn't seem concerned. They said if someone prefers not to be found, that's their right."

"That's just stupid. What if someone took her, like you said?" Just the thought of it creeped Travis out. Not only because she'd been Nathaniel's girlfriend. But that some men were so twisted they'd kidnap women and kids and sell them for sex made him crazy.

"How would you go about looking? It's been over a year now."

"That's a long time."

"I know. It took a while for me to clue in she wasn't coming back. And then longer to get over being hurt and realize it might be something to really worry about. She said her family is from the Spokane area, but do you have any idea how many Johnsons there are? She might as well be a Smith or a Jones for all the help that is."

Travis wanted to believe he'd never have waited this long to go looking for his girl, but Nathaniel wasn't as much a go-getter as the rest of the crew. He was more complacent, eager to please. It took a lot to prod Nathaniel. It hadn't been worth provoking him when they were growing up. Not like Adam or even Noah.

"You called the police. How about hospitals?"

"In the area, yeah. Couldn't get any info."

"Dude, I don't know what to say besides that really sucks big time."

"Do you... do you think God's punishing me?" The guy slumped in his saddle, staring off to the distance.

"Uh, no? God's not like that."

"You sure? Because I knew it was wrong and did it anyway."

"You just described all of humanity."

"I guess. But still."

"Have you asked forgiveness? Because He gives it. Ask me how I know."

"I have, but there's a little piece in my head that keeps asking if it's enough. I know there are consequences. You guys had a baby. My punishment is never seeing Ainsley again."

"That's warped. And I don't think of Toby as punishment. Consequence, yeah, but that's a neutral word, not a good-or-bad word."

"I wish I could be so sure."

"Dude, dig into the Word and do some praying. I will, too. Brothers sticking together and all that."

This time Nathaniel did meet his gaze. "You're claiming me?"

Travis couldn't blame him for hesitating. "Cavanagh strong. Brothers all the way."

DAKOTA HIT TRAVIS'S NUMBER. It went straight to voice-mail. So he and Adam weren't back yet. If Toby wasn't pestering her like a dog with a bone, she'd wait until his dad called to head up the mountain road. But, when he called, it would still take her half an hour to get there.

She should just go. It wouldn't be the first time she'd left Toby with Emma or Alexia, only then she'd been thankful to avoid interacting with Travis.

Not today. Today she wanted to dump her entire load on his broad shoulders and let him take care of everything.

Which meant she needed to hang around Rockstead until he got back.

"Mama!" whined Toby.

Yeah, she should just drive up there. "Is Woody safe in your backpack?"

Her little boy nodded.

She grabbed her purse. "Okay, out to the car then."

"Yay! I go see Daddy."

A few weeks ago, that enthusiasm had soured her. Today, she felt relief. When they were both buckled in, she turned the car toward the highway. Half an hour later, she pulled in beside the Rockstead corral. No Lancaster, so Travis and Adam weren't back yet. Hopefully they wouldn't be much longer.

Emma came running out of the stable and had Toby's door open almost before Dakota put the car in park. "Hi, Toby!"

"Hi, Emma." He grinned at her and let her pull him out of the vehicle.

"I've got his pack, Dakota. I'll watch him until Travis gets back."

Once that was all she'd wanted. Not today, though. "He and Adam were supposed to be back by now. Heard anything?"

"Oh, no one told you? Adam got sick, and Riley took him to Emergency, and he had his appendix out. Nathaniel went with Travis."

"No, I didn't know." There were probably lots of things she was unaware of, and why should anyone bother to inform her? The family at the ranch all knew each other's business. She was an outsider.

The girl scowled. "And no one would take Alexia and me to the fairgrounds on Wednesday. We begged and begged."

Dakota believed it. Declan would never give in to that sort of whining.

A door slammed over at the ranch house across the yard and a woman all dressed up in a royal blue pantsuit shook her fist in Declan's face.

Dakota hadn't even noticed the ritzy looking car over there when she drove in. "Who's that?"

Emma rolled her eyes. "That's Dad's first wife. I hear they never did get along."

Travis's mother? The woman had left when he was a preteen. As far as Dakota knew, she hadn't been seen since. "What's she doing here today?"

"Get off this property and stay away!" Declan's voice was loud and fierce. "There's nothing for you here."

The sound of hoofbeats caused Dakota to turn the other direction as three horses and two riders rounded the curve from the cabins. Travis. He looked dusty and weary, sagging a little in the saddle.

"Daddy!" yelled Toby. Good thing he knew better than to run toward the horses.

Good thing Dakota knew the same.

Travis grinned toward them before catching sight of the woman. His mother. He straightened, and the smile vanished from his face in less time than a blink. He turned in at the corral, keeping his rigid back to the woman as he dismounted.

"Travis?"

Dakota would have expected to hear the woman's

approach, but she hadn't. She reached for Toby and swung him up to her hip.

"Who dat, Mama?"

"Shh."

But the woman turned, her eyes narrowing at the sight of the little boy. "Who's this we have here?"

"Leave him alone." Travis pivoted, his voice harsh and clear.

"Travis. Son. I need to talk to you." She hesitated, looking between them. "Give your mother a moment."

"You are Monica. You are not my mother. You may have happened to give birth to me, but a mother loves her kid and sticks around. You mean nothing to me, as I have clearly meant nothing to you for sixteen years."

Dakota had heard and seen all kinds of moods out of Travis, but never this cold, dead one. She took a step back from the sheer force of it.

"Daddy?"

"Is this your child, Travis? He looks like you."

Fire flared in his eyes. "None of your business."

"I'm his grandmother."

"You're not. You're nothing to him. You gave up any rights a long time ago."

"I'm here to explain. To tell you and your brothers what happened. To make things right."

"You can't," Travis all but snarled.

Monica's narrowed gaze took in Nathaniel and then Emma before riveting back on Toby. When she held out her hands to the boy and took a step closer, Dakota clenched him tight.

Declan stepped between his ex and Dakota. "You've overstayed your welcome."

Monica peered around him to Travis. "Son?"

"You are *not* my mother."

The force of his rebuttal sent a chill through Dakota, reminding her of years gone by. Sure, the woman had hurt him badly, but wasn't forgiveness a thing? Or at least a willingness to listen and reserve final judgment?

"I live in Jewel Lake now. I can be patient. I'll see you again." She gave a smile to Toby that looked more like a grimace. "And you, too, my little boo."

In two seconds, Travis had crossed the gap and plucked Toby out of Dakota's arms. "Don't you come anywhere near my child," he snarled. Then he shouldered past his father, grabbed Lancaster's bridle, and strode into the stable.

They all stared after him.

"Well, I—"

"Get off this ranch, Monica." Declan's voice thundered. "You can't fix what you've done."

Wasn't God all about second chances? Sure, Declan shouldn't welcome Monica back with open arms. He'd been married to Kathryn for a long time now, and they had two girls together. But Travis. How could he reject his mother's overtures without any hint of compassion?

This was the old Travis. The one who'd given Dakota an ultimatum four years ago. The one she'd left behind without a backward glance.

Just like his mother had done.

CHAPTER EIGHTEEN

Y ou okay, Trav?"

Shaking with fury, he led Lancaster into his box stall and set Toby on the rail gate before turning to Dakota. Too bad she'd seen all that. Too bad his son had. "Do I look like it?" The chill in his heart poured out in his voice. It was all he could do to clutch the ice when it wanted to flare into an inferno instead.

She stood by the gate, her arm tightening around Toby. "Not really."

Travis shrugged. "Then there's your answer." He reached for the cinch strap and loosened it. Why wouldn't she go away and leave him to his anger? But no.

"Talk to me."

What did it matter? He'd gotten over his mother — Monica — once before. He'd do it again, and the sooner, the better. "Forget it. It's none of your business." She needed to leave before he lost his temper. Again.

"Trav." The sawdust floor covering nearly hid the sound of her footsteps, but then she touched his sleeve.

He yanked away. "Not now," he ground out.

"Well, sor-*ree*."

"Dakota—"

"No, you listen to me. What you're doing is how a guy gets ulcers. Talk to me. Dump it out."

There was no way she meant that. She knew what could happen. He didn't look at her, just thumbed toward Toby. His kid definitely didn't need to hear.

Travis's blood throbbed in his ears and a reddish sheen covered everything he looked at. If he said one more thing, he was going to explode, and that wouldn't be pretty.

That woman who called herself his mother was lucky he hadn't broke training and punched her one. *That* was how a guy got rid of emotions. Wrestling things. Shoving them. Beating them to pulp in the dirt. It had worked for him and his brothers, stepbrothers included.

But even Declan had drilled into them never to hit a woman. Punching Monica would probably send Travis straight to hell. Even if she didn't act like a mother.

Since he couldn't do that, he'd do the next best thing, which definitely was not a heart-to-heart chit-chat with Dakota or anyone else. Sometimes he accomplished relief with a long, punishing ride, but Lancaster was too weary after three days in the north ranges.

"Leave Toby with the girls. I'm grabbing the ATV and heading out."

Dakota hesitated, a frown crossing her face. "You're *what?*"

Man, she sounded hurt. Confused. He couldn't handle her emotions on top of his own. Just couldn't. He finished unsaddling and yelled, "Nat, can you rub Lancaster down? And call Emma for Toby?"

"Sure, man. Right after Kingpin."

Travis cast a quick glance at his wide-eyed son as he edged past them and strode away. He was just barely holding onto his temper. Onto his grief. He grabbed the key ring from the office wall.

Dakota called his name.

He ignored her. This wasn't how he wanted her to see him. She didn't need to hear the rage and hostility he could barely keep from gushing out of his mouth. Not again. Toby certainly didn't.

He swung onto the four-wheeler and zipped across behind Monica's car, scattering gravel. She and Declan stood in the middle of the parking area, yelling at each other by the looks of their stances. Thankfully, the revved engine of the all-terrain vehicle blocked their words. He'd heard them all before, anyway.

Travis understood Declan. He was his father's son. They settled things with harsh words and punishing work. Blind avoidance helped if you couldn't pummel situations into submission.

He roared the ATV down the trail then cut through the woods to the riverbank. The water seemed low enough. He gunned the machine across. The tires slid on the wet rocks, caught by the current, before finding traction and climbing the steep bank on the other side.

Travis stopped and jumped off, staring down at the water, his breath still heaving. "God, why?" he shouted. "Why?" He lifted a huge rock and heaved it down to the river where it crashed with a mighty splash. The water immediately formed a new route around it.

He threw another rock, then another. The same thing happened.

"Why can't I be a river?" he yelled. Nothing bothered it for more than a fraction of a second. "Why do people need to have stupid feelings?"

His vision blurred.

Now he was *crying*? That was so dumb. His mother — no, Monica — had left years ago when he was just a little kid. He'd been over her for a long time.

Except he wasn't. That was painfully obvious.

"I hate her!" he yelled into the churning current. "Mothers should be for loving, and I hate mine."

Look at him. He was the product of a cold, unfeeling father and an emotionally manipulative mother. How could he possibly think he might do a better job parenting Toby when he'd had no positive examples? He didn't know how. He needed to give his son fully to Dakota. Send more child support.

Except Dakota's family was just as dysfunctional as Travis's. Her parents had stuck together, but they shouldn't have. Any veneer of love and respect had worn off completely over the years. And Travis wouldn't let his brain start on Scotty. The guy was a festering abscess on the face of the earth.

Travis turned off the four-wheeler and sat on a rock, gazing down at the churning river. His gut felt just the same, a jumbled mess, crashing into rocks, trying desperately to get away but doubling back on itself instead. At least the water would continue to flow downstream and into the Clark Fork and eventually into the Pacific. The rocks didn't slow it for long.

His own mess had nowhere to go, but how could he calm it?

Be still, and know that I am God.

Right. Sounded so easy, but it was not. If God really loved him, wouldn't He have given him parents who got along and raised him in faith? Declan had only sent his unruly, unmothered brood to church to get them out of his hair Sunday mornings so he could have coffee with his rancher buddies in peace. Then when Kathryn and her sons had come along, she'd kicked up the religious training a few notches.

At some point, faith had become something Travis clung to, but a fat lot of good that had done. God hadn't fixed anything. Declan was still as harsh as ever. His second wife, Kathryn, had withdrawn, unable to handle her husband any more than his first one had. She just reacted differently.

And Dakota... she was a product of her environment, too. Toby would grow up just as wrecked as Travis.

There was no hope. Second chances were nothing but an illusion.

"Why, God?" But the demanding rage had gone out of his voice. Only bleakness remained.

"Mama, I want Daddy!" Toby hadn't stopped begging and sobbing from his car seat in the back of the car the entire way down from Rockstead.

"I know, buddy." Somehow Dakota kept from snapping at him. It wasn't her son's fault his father had tipped over the edge. That his paternal grandparents had screamed their anger in front of him. And Travis thought she'd just leave their little boy with a traumatized thirteen-year-old in that environment while he went off in a rage for who knew how long? *Think again, buster.*

Not this mama. She was going to protect Toby from that kind of drama every moment while she had breath in her body.

She'd had stuff to tell Travis. Little details like she didn't have a job anymore. Things he needed to know if they were going to keep having any sort of relationship.

So much for the fantasies she'd indulged in as she'd driven up the ranch lane earlier. She'd dreamed Travis held her close and told her not to worry about anything, that he'd take care of her.

Right. She'd been kidding herself. He couldn't handle his own emotions any better than he had four years ago. What kind of a role model was he? No better than Declan or Monica. And, sadly, no better than Dakota's parents or brother, either.

Looked like Sage was right, after all. People didn't really change. And that meant Dakota was Toby's last and only hope for growing up without all the garbage in his family tree weighing him down.

Which meant she needed to return the call to the store in Butte and agree to an interview. She'd had three days to stew while Travis was in the back country, plenty of time to search job openings online. This one was the best fit for her experience and education… or lack of it.

It felt underhanded to take Toby from everyone and everything he knew, but it was for his own good. Thank the Lord she and Travis had handled custody on their own without a court order. He would totally be furious with her. She could already hear the venom in his voice… and that would only prove her point.

Dakota clenched the steering wheel. She didn't want her point proved. She wanted to sink back into the daydreams she'd been having over the past several weeks, where Travis loved her, gently but fiercely, and they were united as a family and Toby had a safe, healthy place to grow up.

Toby was still sobbing when they hit Jewel Lake town limits.

Would Travis come to town and have it out with her when he discovered she hadn't left Toby with Emma? Probably. She shuddered at the memory of his rage. No way could she let him catch up to her and Toby. That meant she needed to park the car a few blocks away, maybe in an out-of-the-way cul-de-sac. She'd keep the doors to the townhouse locked and the lights out and pray Travis wouldn't figure out she was home, after all.

Pray. Yeah. She ought to do some of that. She could use a boatload of wisdom like the book of James talked about. But hadn't she been asking? She had. Unless they'd just been words she didn't mean, while she let her heart and emotions believe a fairytale was truth.

Possibly guilty.

"Mama!" Toby's wails increased when he realized they weren't parked at home.

"Shush, baby." She swung him to her hip and reached back in for his backpack and the ever-present Woody toy. Then she locked the car and headed toward home, carrying a kicking little boy and losing her patience. Maybe she'd lost that an hour ago.

Of course, Sage was just pulling in from work when Dakota rounded the last corner.

Sage stood beside her car door twirling her keys and watching Dakota's approach. "What's going on? Why isn't he...?"

Bless her friend for not finishing the question. "Long story."

"It must be. Did your car break down again?"

Dakota blinked. "No, it's fine. I just needed to park it somewhere so no one would think I was home."

"No one... ah... do you want to come in? I stopped by the diner and grabbed takeout from my mom. Pulled pork. She always thinks I'm about to starve to death, so she put in plenty."

Sage's parents owned the Golden Grill, and the food was amazing. But Dakota's gut was churning so hard anything she put in would likely come straight back up. It might settle Toby, though. She hadn't planned on having him around for supper tonight, since he was always with Travis on weekends. "Sure. Thanks."

Her friend's place was a mirror-image to hers. She set Toby down and handed him his backpack. He glowered at her with an expression so much like his daddy's that Dakota nearly started bawling herself.

"Hey, Toby, I have Toy Story 5. Want to watch it?"

Toby whipped to face their neighbor. "Okay. Me and Woody." He unzipped the pack and tugged out his favorite toy. With one more scowl at his mother, he settled on the sofa, clenching his stuffie to his chest while Sage got the movie started.

"You can even eat supper at the coffee table," Sage offered conspiratorially. "I know Mama doesn't usually let you, but I bet it's okay tonight."

Thanks for undermining me. But Dakota didn't say it out loud. It would certainly be easier to dump everything on her friend if she was sure her son was occupied. She helped Sage dish up the coleslaw and meat and brought a bowl to Toby along with a cup of iced tea.

"As for you, sit." Sage pointed at a chair by the kitchen table. "Let me pray." She didn't wait for Dakota's response. "Dear Lord, thank You for this food, and thank You Mom sent enough to feed us all. I pray for Dakota and whatever the situation is, that You will give wisdom, strength, comfort… whatever it is she needs. In Jesus' name, amen."

Whatever she needed. A miracle, for starters. "I don't even know where to start."

"The beginning?"

"I lost my job this week. And also Toby's daycare space since I was late picking him up one too many times, but that doesn't even matter since I don't have a job."

Sage's fork had been halfway to her mouth, but she set it back down. "No way. Why didn't you tell me?"

"I don't know. I guess I hoped Travis would make good on the hints he's been giving lately about getting back together, and all that mess wouldn't matter."

"You can't count on—"

"Trust me, I've figured that out." A little late, but better than *too* late. "He was away on a trail ride for a few days, so I was going to talk to him when I dropped Toby off this afternoon." She glanced into the other room, but her son seemed entirely focused on the movie.

"Uh huh…"

"Travis's mother showed up. It honestly seemed to me like she was trying to apologize for walking out the way she had, but he shut her down. Then she and Declan got into a shouting match, and Travis looked about ready to explode and took off on a four-wheeler. He told me to leave Toby with Emma. While Declan and Monica were yelling obscenities at each other twenty feet away."

"Oh, no."

"So, I brought him home. And I have no idea what to do next, because I can't let Toby be in that kind of toxic environment. Not that my family is any better. With no job, no daycare — Sage, I'm at my wits' end. I'd put so much trust in the fact that Travis seemed to have changed." Too late, she remembered Sage's opinions on that.

"The thing that stands out to me is that you put your trust in Travis, when only Jesus could solve the problem. People don't really change. Not that much. Neither does Jesus, but that turns out to be a good thing. He's the same yesterday, today, and tomorrow. And He knows your mess, sweetie. He has a solution."

"I do actually believe that." Dakota covered her face with her hands. "But I feel like a marble in a pinball machine, whacked every which way. Not in control."

"Control is a delusion."

Said the woman who refused to relinquish it. But even so, Dakota could see her friend was right. All she could do was trust God. But could she hand over her hopes and dreams and plans?

CHAPTER NINETEEN

Travis parked the ATV beside the fuel tanks. On auto, he poured gas into the nearly-empty machine. The rule was to keep the tanks full in case of emergency. It was only common sense.

Like he was a fount of that today.

"Dude, where have you been?"

Still pressing the gas nozzle, Travis turned slightly to see Nathaniel. "Out for a ride."

"You're covered in mud."

"Yup." That would be from all the creeks he'd revved through. He was spattered completely and soaked from the waist down. Cleaning the leather of his cowboy boots was going to be a major chore. Whatever.

Travis hung the gas hose and tightened the cap on the ATV's fuel tank before glancing casually around. Monica's car was gone. So was Dakota's. He should only feel relief, but the turmoil was not completely gone from his gut. "Where's Emma?"

Nathaniel frowned. "In the house. Why?"

"She has Toby." He took a few steps that direction then realized no one would let his soaked, muddy self through the door.

"No, she doesn't."

Travis whipped around and pinned his stepbrother with a glare. "What do you mean, she doesn't?"

"Plain English, dude. Emma doesn't have Toby, because Dakota took him with her."

"She *what?*" The reddish sheen that had barely faded swelled again.

"Stop asking stupid questions."

Travis reached to shove Nathaniel, but the other guy stepped out of the way with his hands up. Right. Pounding out his stepbrother wouldn't solve anything. It would feel really good for about five minutes, though. No. Travis dropped his hands to his sides. "Sorry."

Nathaniel eyed him warily. "Accepted. But the person you need to apologize to is Dakota."

"Why?"

"Are you that dumb? You terrified her. Declan and Monica yelled at each other with words no woman or child should have to hear. Toby was crying. And the guy who supposedly cares for them flips into a rage and runs away?"

"Supposedly?" Travis bumped his chest against Nathaniel's. "Why do you think I left? I was protecting them."

"Dude, that's stupid."

Travis shoved. Not hard, but enough to get the guy's attention. "Call me that again, and I'll *stupid* you."

Nathaniel, who'd staggered back, stepped right back in. "Listen to yourself."

"I am. I was about to completely lose it in front of Toby and Dakota. They didn't need to see me struggling like that. I had to get control of myself."

"So, you deserted them in the middle of a yelling match. Did you really expect Dakota to abandon Toby and go on her way?"

Not when Nathaniel put it that way, no. The tinge of rage thinned slightly. Travis grimaced. "I didn't think how it would look to her."

"You didn't think. Period."

A few years ago, that would have earned Nathaniel a punch in the jaw. Now, the words slipped through a crack in Travis's anger and resonated. His stepbrother was right. He'd only thought of himself, not Dakota. Not Toby. His motive had been sort of okay — not wanting to explode in front of them — but he'd gone about it all wrong.

He was such a screwup.

Travis rubbed his hands through his hair and felt the globules of mud. He needed a shower. Clean clothes. Food — although dinner at the ranch house would have come and gone while he was raging at the river. Cook might have saved him a plate. If not, he'd drive down to Jewel Lake, get some takeout, apologize to Dakota, and bring his son home where he belonged.

He sighed. "Thanks, Nat."

His stepbrother's eyebrows rose. "For…?"

"Helping me see reason."

"Anytime, dude. Praying for you."

Travis calmed a little more. "Appreciated. Obviously, I need God's help."

"We all do." Nathaniel's quick grin faded rapidly as he looked away.

Drat. Travis kept forgetting other people had problems, too. Nathaniel had told him all about Ainsley on their three days of range riding. What would he have done if Dakota had ghosted him like that? He'd have gone ballistic. He'd have tracked her down somehow, no question. He'd have called in a private investigator or something.

Travis gripped Nathaniel's shoulder, this time in solidarity rather than anger. "Praying for you, too. Bro." First time he'd let that word out of his mouth for one of his stepbrothers. "Hey, what's the word on Adam? His truck is still missing."

"Ruptured appendix, so he's still in the hospital, fighting an infection. Sounds like he'll be home soon, though. Maybe tomorrow."

"Okay, good. Those things can be deadly, I hear."

"Yeah. I talked to Riley. She said to thank everyone for praying." Nathaniel chuckled. "Who'd ever thought this family would get on some prayer vigil together, huh?"

Travis grinned. He and Nat had prayed together — out loud, even — for Adam and each member of the family every night they'd been away. They'd even tried to dissect Declan's marriage to Kathryn, but it made no sense. Since their parents obviously needed prayers, though, they'd done that. Through it all, Nathaniel had become Travis's brother, something that sixteen years of sharing a last name and growing up together hadn't accomplished.

Travis gestured to his clothes. "I'm gonna give Dakota a call. Then I'll probably whip down the mountain and get Toby."

"Cook saved you a plate."

"Good, because I'm starved."

Nathaniel chuckled. "You're always starved."

Hard to argue with. Ranching was hard physical labor. A guy ate when he could.

"Thanks again for taking care of Lancaster." Travis turned away, thumbing on his phone while he was still near the house's signal. He tapped Dakota's number. It went straight to voicemail. He frowned, tapped it again, and got the same result. Ditto on the third time. No point leaving a message, as he'd be out of range in a few more steps.

He'd take that shower and change of clothes then come back and try again. Or not. He needed to get Toby, regardless. But… why wasn't Dakota picking up?

DAKOTA EASED the door almost all the way closed, but Toby remained quiet. She went back to Sage's kitchen, where the blinds had been lowered. The drapes were pulled in the living room, too. No one would be able to see in.

She slumped into the sofa where Toby had spent his evening. "Whew. He's finally asleep. I can't thank you enough."

"No problem. The bedroom is just how Lyssa left it when she married Kirk and moved out a couple of months ago. Are you sure you don't want to sleep in there, too? The bed has to be more comfortable than the sofa."

Dakota shook her head. "Toby's never slept with

anyone. He's never even shared a room since he was a few months old. He'll do better by himself."

"If you're sure."

"Yeah. The sofa will be okay. I might just sneak out your back door and into mine to grab my toothbrush and some pajamas, though."

"Can you do that without turning on any lights? There's not much daylight left."

"Sure." She shrugged. "I've lived there for four years, and we don't leave stuff on the floor to trip over. Maybe I should go do that right now. Then it's done."

"You don't think Travis will catch you?"

He'd called nearly an hour ago. Three times. No message. Then nothing.

"If he was coming to town, I'd think he'd already have come, but I haven't heard his truck pull in. It's loud enough I'm sure I'd have heard it." What did that mean? Maybe it meant he was still angry. In her memory, a wooden chair splintered against the wall near her head. She shuddered, and panic swelled.

"Okay. Well, be careful."

Dakota grabbed her keys, silenced her phone and tucked it in her hip pocket, then peered through the back-door window. It was dusk, so the light might come on from the motion sensor. There was no way to turn it off from here, though. About twenty feet separated the two units' doors.

She shook her head and opened the door. Her neighbor was rubbing off on her with all her fear monger-ing. It was like Sage expected the worst and even relished it.

What would happen if Travis caught her? Sage would lock the door. They'd have it out.

Panic tightened in Dakota's chest. He wouldn't hurt her, would he? Had he really changed? She'd begun to think so, but after this afternoon, she couldn't be certain.

Someone was watching out for her. Sage would call the police if necessary.

Still, Dakota hurried across the grass and let herself into her own home, locking the door behind her. She riffled through her room, grabbed her pajamas, her tooth-brush… was there anything else she'd need overnight? Her ereader.

Dakota stepped back into the hallway as headlights flashed in the front windows. Fear surged up her throat.

The doorbell rang. Twice. Three times. Someone knocked on the door. "Dakota! Are you in there?"

She stilled her heart. He didn't actually know if she was present. Her car was parked several blocks away. There were no lights on.

"Dakota!" Frustration came through his voice.

She stood out of his line of vision in her bedroom doorway and waited, ready to dive in either direction.

It didn't take long for knocking to begin on the back door. He called her name again, mounting irritation evident in his voice.

What would happen if she opened the door and talked to him? Could they have a rational discussion like two adult human beings? He'd been so irate.

Her phone buzzed in her pocket. Thank the Lord she'd thought to silence it. A minute later his truck engine started, the lights blazed in again, and then he drove away.

Dakota slid down the wall and took a few shuddering breaths. Oh, good grief, she was crying again. This time there was no one to hear, no one to see. She let it all out in gulping sobs that put her small son's efforts to shame.

"Oh, God, what a mess. I don't know if I did the right thing, but he still seems angry."

She should have taken his call. Then he wouldn't have come to town. She could have told him, firmly but calmly, that he needed to get control of his anger, that she was keeping Toby this weekend for his own safety.

But was that the only reason? It was... wasn't it? Or was she protecting Toby because of her own breaking heart? How was she supposed to separate the issues?

Dakota blew her nose and splashed cold water on her face. She brushed her hair and quickly French braided it for the night. Then she crossed the space back to Sage's, locking both doors behind her.

"I was about to phone you. What a close call! I can't believe he came right then. It's a good thing he didn't catch you."

"Sage?" Dakota waited until her friend made eye contact. "Relax. I'm fine."

"I was just thinking about what you said about the job interview in Butte. I can take a few hours off work — I have unused vacation days — and watch Toby while you drive over. Or we could come along, and I could take him to the park or something."

"You'd do that for me?"

"Sure. That's what friends are for."

It certainly beat the thought of asking Mom to babysit. "I'll call them in the morning, I guess. See what they say.

But I'm not sure moving out of town is the right thing to do. All my support network is in Jewel Lake."

"Except for me, your support net is not very trustworthy."

Also possibly including Sage, though she wasn't completely wrong.

Sage's face brightened. "We could even ask Lyssa and Kirk if you could stay in their apartment for a month or two if you got the job. They're here for the summer, anyway. It probably wouldn't be a big deal, and it would buy you some time to give your notice here and find something over there. And their neighbor is a middle-aged woman with a home daycare. It could all be just perfect."

"Sounds like you want to be rid of me."

"No, never. I love having you next door, and I'm afraid to think who'll move in if you leave. But I can't let that hold you back. The main thing is that you and Toby are safe in a place where you have a good job and can take care of him."

That sounded plausible. Perhaps even right. Dakota reached for her friend and hugged her. "Thanks. I really need to pray about this. It's such a big decision, and I'm so afraid to make the wrong one."

And she needed to be careful whom she trusted.

CHAPTER TWENTY

No, she's not here." Blustering, Dakota's father filled the doorway. "And if she was, I wouldn't tell you. You're nothing but scum. Now get lost."

"But where is she?" Travis tried to see past the man. Surely Dakota's mother was inside somewhere. She might be more accommodating. Right, but she'd never go against her husband. Definitely not in front of him.

Mr. Erickson shrugged as though he didn't care.

It might even be true. He'd never been the sort of daddy where a kid could snuggle on his lap and feel loved. He'd been more like Declan — something Travis and Dakota'd had in common — which was one more reason Travis did his utmost to be the opposite kind of father to Toby. His goal was to break the cycle. He knew what it was like to be a kid no one approved of, one who was yelled at and who'd been cuffed on the side of the head.

Never that for Toby. Only love and protection. Safety. He thought he'd been doing that, so what had been going through Dakota's mind to take their son and hide?

He shouldn't have gone to her parents' place. She wouldn't have trusted them with this. But where was she?

"If you hear from her, please tell her to give me a call. Or phone me yourself. My number's the same as it's always been." Travis said it loud enough for Dakota's mother to hear if she were listening. There was zero chance her dad would do it.

The man cursed. "Get out. If she doesn't want to be around you, then I'm not gonna make her."

"I get Toby on weekends."

"Only because she lets you. Maybe she's wised up. Ever think of that?"

Travis retreated a step. Only because she let him? What was that supposed to mean? Toby was his kid!

Mr. Erickson shut the door rather firmly.

That had been futile. Travis's brain turned those final words over and over. Only because Dakota let him? With a sinking feeling, he realized their arrangement was all verbal. He had no legal backup. Yes, he could file against her, and he'd win, but it might take a while.

Why was she avoiding him like this? Didn't she see he'd driven away to protect her and Toby from his anger? He'd never hurt her. If she'd been in an accident — driven off the ranch lane, or something — he'd have seen the evidence. It was like she'd disappeared into thin air as totally as Nathaniel's ex had, but taking Toby with her.

Travis prowled aimlessly around Jewel Lake, up one street, down another. He couldn't simply drive home and pretend it didn't matter. He had to fight for his son. Toby needed him, needed two parents, even if they didn't share a household.

That's why he'd pushed the arrangement on Dakota when they split up. She'd laughed, sure he'd give up when he had to wrangle a six-month-old by himself for forty-eight hours. It had been hard, but he'd done it. His kid was worth not sleeping for two nights a week. Worth the diaper stench. Worth everything. And it had gotten easier in the past couple of years.

He turned down another street a few blocks from Dakota's. Then the so-called truce had gotten his hopes up — wait a second. That was Dakota's car parked in a cul-de-sac of seniors' housing. Was she visiting someone here? Like whom?

Travis backed up, turned in, and stopped behind the car. He got out and peered into it. Yes, there was Toby's other car seat. Her thermal mug. He looked around the neighborhood. It was well past dusk now. Looked like most people were home, except the house beside them was unlit and had a *for sale* sign out front.

He rubbed the back of his neck. He was not going to go knocking on every door in this neighborhood. If she'd parked here... he turned and looked toward her townhouse. Hmm. It wouldn't be a long walk, not with the playground between that she could cut through. So the evidence was that she'd parked here and hiked home with Toby. Then hid out and refused to answer the door when he'd been out front.

Unless she was at Sage's. But she would have heard or seen him, anyway. The front doors were right next to each other.

So that meant it wasn't an accident she hadn't picked up his calls. It wasn't likely that her cell phone battery had run out. Dakota was far too organized to let that happen. It meant she was purposefully, willfully avoiding him.

He drove around and parked in her driveway again. The lights were still out. Next door, too, but it was only ten o'clock. He tapped her number one more time. Voicemail again. This time he left a message.

"Dakota, I know you're home. I saw your car. What I don't know is why you're avoiding me. I mean, I get the situation wasn't ideal when you came up to Rockstead." Now there was an understatement. "How about you come outside, and we talk this out like two rational adults? I promise I just want to take Toby for the weekend." Well, that was a barefaced lie. He also wanted Dakota, but if he could only have one pick, he had to choose in favor of his son.

Travis ended the message and set the phone down on the console. He tapped his fingers against the steering wheel and waited. What was he going to do if she ignored this message, too?

It wasn't like he was going to sleep tonight with this unresolved, and if he were going to not-sleep, it might as well be right here in the truck as in his cabin at the ranch. He tilted his seat back a few inches and angled his cowboy hat to partially cover his face. Not so far he couldn't keep an eye on both front doors, though.

If she was worried about what the neighbors would think with his truck there all night, she'd come out soon and set him straight to get him to move along.

He'd wait.

"He's not going anywhere." Sage peered between the slats of the breakfast nook's mini-blinds. "Looks like he's settling in for a long winter's nap."

Dakota sat on the sofa, face in her hands. Travis was stubborn enough to spend the night right there. She had two choices. Grab Toby, head out the backdoor to the car, and drive away — but where would she go... and why? Or she could be an adult and go outside and talk to Travis.

He'd been super angry up at the ranch. His message half an hour ago had only sounded frustrated. He'd calmed right down in this last message, though there was still a slight edge to his voice.

He wasn't going to hurt her. Was he? After all her childhood memories of how violent her father got when he was in a rage, her first reaction was self-defense, but Travis had never given her reason to fear for her safety. Except that last night up at the ranch when Toby was a baby. Right now, the memory was strong.

Was he still that guy? Was his reformation only a coverup?

She rose from the sofa and walked toward the door. "I'm going to go talk to him. Lock the door behind me. He's going to want Toby, but don't let him in."

Sage's eyes widened. "You can't do that."

"If you've got a better idea, tell me right now."

"Call him to the door. Keep it locked between you. I'm afraid for you. For Toby."

Dakota took a deep breath. Probably a good idea. Travis's voice might have calmed, but that only made it cold, controlled. She fired off a text.

"I'm ready to call the police if he seems violent."

Fear surged again. She steadied her breathing again. Nodded.

The truck door shut. Had he slammed it? Maybe? Or maybe she was just jittery. How could she know?

She peered through the peephole as Travis approached. He placed both hands on the door and closed his eyes for a minute. Praying? She should do the same.

"Where's Toby?"

Was his voice extra gruff? So hard to know. "Asleep."

"It's Friday. He's mine on the weekend."

"You abandoned him."

"I did not. You were there. Emma was there. You had no right to take him."

"I had every right and responsibility to take him to a safe environment."

He tipped his hat back, his dark eyes narrowing in on the peephole. So much for thinking she'd overreacted. He was the one overreacting. He'd started it.

"You scared the living daylights out of both of us when you went all incommunicado and ripped out of there. Your parents were yelling curses at each other. Emma hopped on Desiree and shot up the trail, bareback. What was I supposed to do? Stand there in that toxic environment and wait for you to come back with your smiley-face intact? You don't even have one. I should have remembered."

Travis winced and took a step back.

Good. He needed to hear her, loud and clear. "Toby was terrified. He cried the whole way to town. I hope that satisfies you."

"I just want him." But his voice had softened.

"You can't have him, Travis Cavanagh. He's finally sleeping."

"I'll stay right here, and take him in the morning."

"No." She put her hands on her hips, not that he could see her stance. "I have one job in life, and that's to protect my son. Until you can prove to me you're not going to endanger or abandon him, I'm not leaving you alone with him. Especially not at that awful ranch."

"Excuse me?" The gentler tone was gone.

Where was that place they'd been last week, where fantasies became real? The place where she believed she was still in love with this man and he with her, that they could overcome anything.

Because… they could not overcome everything. Not if Travis couldn't overcome his anger. Not if she couldn't trust him.

He leaned into the peephole and glared at her from one eye. "You have no right to keep him from me."

"I do." Dakota's voice trembled. "You can explain that to the police."

Sage bumped Dakota's hip, eyebrows raised, fingers on her phone. Ready to dial.

Dakota shook her head. They weren't there.

Travis moved away from the door. His hands dropped to his side and fisted as he shook his head. "You're killing me here, Dakota. I'm sorry, okay? Did you ever stop to think what it looked like from my side? I haven't seen Monica since I was twelve, and there she was, right when I got back from a grueling three days in the back country. When she realized Toby was my son, I freaked out. It was the last thing I ever wanted her to know."

Dakota drew herself to full height and crossed her arms in front of her. "So, you ran away."

"Declan taught me never to punch a woman."

She angled her head. Had she heard him right?

"I was so tempted. Not you. My mother. I didn't trust myself."

"I didn't trust you, either. I still don't."

He rubbed his face with both hands. "Dakota, I'm sorry. I didn't want to lose my temper in front of you. In front of Toby. I only tried to protect him."

"Do you know how many times I saw my dad lose it in front of me as a kid?"

"I know. You've told me." He looked away, his jaw tensing. "Declan did, too. Believe me, I never want Toby to experience that."

"Then you know what? You need to grow up. Get some counseling. Figure things out. Because I don't want Toby to experience it, either."

"Dakota, sweetie, we're on the same page. We can work this out."

She shook her head. "We're not on the same page. I'm going to keep Toby away from you until you prove you've got a handle on this." She held up her hand. "I know you can get a court order. But you know what? I can get a restraining order."

He laughed, the sound harsh. "You can't be serious. You have a job here. A home. A family."

"I *had* a job. If you weren't so full of yourself, I'd have been able to talk to you this afternoon and tell you I got fired a few days ago. It doesn't even matter why anymore.

And Toby won't be in daycare anymore, either, so don't think you can get him from there."

"You lost your job? Man, that sucks. I'm sorry."

"Me, too."

"Let me help you. Let me—"

"No. I don't trust you, remember?" And she was remembering all the reasons why.

"What are you going to do?"

"I'm not completely sure. I have some ideas, but you know what? I'm not sharing them with you. Because my highest priority is keeping Toby safe."

He rubbed his hands across his neck. "If you think I'd hurt him, you're crazy."

"You already hurt him." Dakota's heart broke inside her. She couldn't back down. Couldn't trust him. Just couldn't.

CHAPTER TWENTY-ONE

Travis drove slowly away from his son. Away from the woman he loved but who infuriated him.

Did he have an anger problem? Well, yeah. Wouldn't anyone who'd lived his life? Look at the way masculinity had been modeled for him. Travis figured he'd come a long way considering Declan's parenting.

He angled his truck up the ranch lane. If Dakota wouldn't see reason tonight, he'd get some sleep and drive down again in the morning. He'd wear her down. He needed Toby. He needed her. He couldn't just give up.

He loved her. He'd only been trying to protect them both.

No. She was right. He'd only been thinking of himself. Of what his parents were like and how what they were doing affected him. But could he help the hole in his heart where parents who loved each other and their sons should have resided?

What was he trying to fill that hole with, anyway? Because nothing Declan or Monica did now could repair the damage. Even if they each performed a one-eighty personality change, fell in love, and tried to rebuild all they'd torn down. That would mean Kathryn's exit, of course, and Travis's stepbrothers. It would mean Alexia and Emma would experience a broken home, not that what they had was much better.

So, no. The past could not be repaired. His future was up to him. What mattered was how he overcame it. And hadn't he been trying? He'd delved into Scripture and tried to find his anchor there. He'd agreed to Dakota's truce.

None of it was good enough.

He'd slipped up once — he still didn't think it was that bad, what he'd done — and wham. Up went Dakota's walls again, higher than ever. Probably God saw him as a loser, too. Someone who didn't deserve another chance.

"God? Is that true?" Travis heard the catch in his voice, but he didn't much care. If God'd had enough of Travis's failures, too, he didn't know how he'd bear it. How did people live without hope?

I will never leave you nor forsake you.

Well, that was a start. "God, show me what to do. Everything I've tried to figure out has blown up in my face. Is it just because I've done what I thought was best without asking You? But… it seemed so obvious."

Through his broken thoughts and prayers, he made his way back up the mountain road. After he parked his truck, he walked to his cabin, empty without his young son. Yes, Toby's room was always vacant five nights of the week, but this was Friday. Toby should be inside, wearing cowboy pajamas, hugging his Woody toy, dreaming of barrel races on Clover.

It was one thing to lose Dakota again. Their relationship had been on-again-off-again for years. Yes, he'd definitely hoped this time they'd make it through the hard parts and commit to loving each other for life, but maybe, in the dark recesses of his mind, he'd known it couldn't last.

But losing access to Toby? That was absolutely unthinkable. Dakota was right. He'd go to the courthouse on Monday and file against her. But she'd countered and threatened a restraining order.

He didn't deserve that. He wasn't a threat to her or their son. He wasn't.

She didn't trust him. She was afraid of him.

How could he have let that happen?

Travis slumped onto his camp chair and stared out at the ranch. The yard lights, sensing no motion, went dark. Stars by the millions dotted the moonless sky. Over in the stables, a horse whiffled. An owl hooted across the meadow.

He inhaled deeply as though he could bring all that peace inside along with oxygen.

"Trav?" Nathaniel's voice.

"Yeah. What're you doing up?"

"It's not that late. Just past midnight. I was kinda watching for you."

Travis's heart warmed just a little. "Thanks."

"Did you get the little guy?"

"No." Travis leaned forward, rubbing his face with both hands. "Seems Dakota's afraid I can't control my temper. That I'll hurt him."

"Ouch."

Travis swallowed the lump in his throat. "She doesn't get that's exactly *why* I escaped. To protect him."

"Uh huh."

"So... I dunno. What's the right wait to deal with anger? Sometimes it just flares up out of nowhere, like this afternoon. You and me, we'd just got back from the north ranges. We'd had a decent trip, and I was looking forward to seeing Dakota and Toby. And then Monica was here..."

"Did you ever call her mom?"

Travis shrugged. "When I was a little kid. But she ceased to be my mother when she left us. That's not what moms do." Nathaniel was quiet so long that Travis couldn't help continuing. "Right? Moms are loving and kind. Sure, they discipline their kids, but they're there for them."

"I don't know, man. I'm no expert in relationships." A bitter laugh came from Nathaniel. "But I think you need to forgive her. Forgive your dad, too."

Travis chuckled harshly.

Nathaniel remained silent.

"You really think that?" Because his stepbrother hadn't laughed with him. The idea was ludicrous. "I think people have to be sorry before they're forgiven. There's an order to things."

"I think you're wrong, bro. I've been really struggling with this because of Ainsley. She ghosted me. She certainly hasn't told me she's sorry. But hanging onto my frustration and anger has been killing my gut. It's been interfering with praying. It's messed *me* up, inside."

"So, you've forgiven her?" It still didn't make sense.

Nathaniel sighed. "About a hundred times. It doesn't

seem to stick, but I know it's what I need to do. I've been talking to Eli—"

"I thought he was the youth pastor. You know, for the teens."

"He's about our age, give or take. He's become a friend, and he's taken a bunch of counseling courses. Anyway, yeah, I've been talking to him."

"Huh." Travis leaned back in his chair. Why hadn't he thought of getting help? Because he hated admitting he wasn't in control, that's why. Because Travis Cavanagh was a tough cowboy who could do anything, he set his mind to or he'd know the reason why. "Has it helped?"

"Yeah. It's hard, though, you know what I mean?"

Did he ever.

"This whole forgiveness thing. It's like God. There's nothing He won't forgive."

"But we have to ask."

"True, but it's already covered. The asking is for our own sake. So, look at Ainsley. I can forgive her, at least on a good day. But for her to experience that, she needs to come to me and be sorry. Does that make sense?"

"Kinda. But would you really just welcome her back with open arms if she did that?"

"God does."

"Dude, you're not God."

Nathaniel laughed. "Thanks for noticing."

But wouldn't Travis welcome Dakota back to his arms in a blink if she apologized for what she'd said tonight? Still, she hadn't forgiven him. Maybe because he'd assumed she would. Pretty much demanded it.

He was a mess.

"I think it would take some time to regain trust," Nathaniel said pensively. "But I couldn't reject her apology out of hand. Not when I call myself a Jesus-follower."

Trust. Yeah, Travis had broken Dakota's trust. And then she'd broken his by holding Toby out of reach. Nathaniel was right. Travis needed to figure out how to forgive her and deal with his own issues so he'd be ready to get to the restoration part. Could he get all that done overnight?

"How did the interview go?" Sage asked as soon as Dakota entered the playground.

"I don't know. It would be so different. I'm not sure I can do this." Dakota swung Toby into her arms and kissed his face until he giggled.

"Is it different in a bad way?"

"I'm not talking about the details in front of my little buddy. How about we get some ice cream before we head back to Jewel Lake?"

"Ice cream!" Toby squealed.

"I thought you might agree." Dakota lowered him to the ground and took his hand. "What did you and Woody and Miss Sage do?"

"Woody slided."

"Did Toby slide, too?"

He shook his head, eyes wide. For a kid who galloped his pony around the arena with no fear, he sure didn't like the whoosh of a kiddie slide, but there was plenty of time for him to grow up.

Dakota was in no hurry for him to become a teenager

and then, eventually, leave her behind. Even heading off to preschool in a few weeks was almost more than she could bear.

Oh, no. If she moved to Butte, she'd have to cancel that, too. How could she possibly figure out the right thing to do? She was praying. Constantly. But so far, she hadn't seen any writing in the sky.

Oh, Lord, help me know, she prayed for what must have been the hundredth time today.

She got Toby a bubblegum ice cream in a cup while she and Sage enjoyed mint chocolate chip cones. She probably shouldn't have sprung for a treat like this, not without a job, but it wasn't that pricy. Somehow, they'd survive this mess.

God's got it. He always had. He always would. It would be nice if He let her in on His plan, though. She hated being patient. She hated the not knowing. It wasn't just for her. It was for Toby, too.

She could always go to Travis and talk it out. But... could she? Would he talk to her without yelling? Would he forgive her? Welcome her back in?

That was the problem. The past few weeks had seemed to be too good to be true. It was like she'd subconsciously been waiting for the other boot to drop. For the old Travis to appear, so she could comfort herself that he was the same guy he'd been back then. She'd been waiting for him to prove it was all about him. He'd done that by charging off in a rage and leaving her to shield Toby's ears from his yelling grandparents. Hadn't he?

"Penny for your thoughts." Sage licked her ice cream and looked at Dakota inquisitively.

Dakota glanced at Toby and shook her head. Sage could be curious all she wanted, but Toby was never going to overhear his mom dissecting her relationship with his dad. It simply wasn't going to happen.

Half an hour later, though, his gaping mouth and gentle snores from his car seat while Woody drooped to the seat beside him changed that.

Dakota looked over at Sage. "I don't think the job is a good fit, but I just don't know what to do in Jewel Lake. I wish I'd gone to college, but it seems too late for that now."

"Never too late."

"How, with a kid who's dependent on me? I need a job now, not in four years."

"I get that, but you can take all kinds of things via distance learning. What degree would you want?"

Dakota passed a slow-moving motorhome on the interstate and pulled back into the right lane. "Honestly? I'm not sure. I've felt so trapped that I've never really looked into it. And I liked my job well enough. At least, until I didn't."

"And then you began to think you and Travis would get back together, and you'd move up to Rockstead."

"Maybe? But even if we loved each other enough to make it work, living at the ranch wouldn't be ideal. Rockstead was once a dude ranch when Travis's grandparents owned it. Those six little cabins were for tourists, not for families to live in permanently. They don't have real kitchens, for one thing."

"Aren't Riley and Adam living in one of them?"

"For now. But they're hoping to move into the house at Running Creek sometime soon. That's where Adam's parents lived."

"I remember."

It was hard to guess what Sage knew. She asked so many questions. "Anyway, they have a plan of sorts in place, so they're looking at the cabin as temporary. And… they don't have a four-year-old."

Also, the rumor Mrs. McDiarmid had cited of Riley's pregnancy didn't seem to be true. Dakota hadn't bothered to ask, and Travis hadn't said. If the information became public, she'd find out then. She wasn't like Sage, needing the inside track on everyone else's life.

"That just proves Travis wasn't serious about you this summer."

What on earth? Dakota shot her passenger a questioning look.

"If he was, he'd have been making plans for where you'd live after you were married."

"Just because we hadn't gotten to that point yet doesn't mean he wasn't serious." Those kisses, those lingering looks, they had to mean something. There was no way he'd been performing, putting on a good show to pull her back in, just so he could be the one to reject her this time.

No. It was Dakota who'd asked for the truce. It hadn't been his idea at all.

Could he be thinking *she'd* been the one to toy with his emotions?

CHAPTER TWENTY-TWO

W hat, no little shadow this morning?" Eli gripped Travis's hand at the end of the church service with a questioning smile.

"Not today." Travis glanced behind him, but most of the crowd had already left, and no one was waiting to talk to Eli. "Do you have some free time? Nathaniel says you've got a good listening ear, and I could use some advice."

"I've got a few hours right now, if you want to catch lunch. I'm due at the Simpsons for dinner later." Eli grimaced. "They're sure if I spend more time with their daughter, we'll fall in love."

Travis couldn't help the grin. "Stephanie? Can't see it working out."

"Right? But a young, single pastor is apparently fair game. I can't even imagine what it must have been like for men like me in years past. There was a real stigma against single pastors and teachers, like they needed the community to help solve their pathetic status."

"I had no idea." Yeah, maybe he could get along with Eli.

The guy seemed down-to-earth with a sense of humor. "I can grab takeout for us if you want. What would you like?"

Eli searched Travis's face. "I'll accept that offer. Call into the Golden Grill and ask Estelle to put on a Pastor Eli special. She knows what I like. Then meet me back here. There's a log on the trail by the creek with my name on it." He pointed toward the park next to the church.

"Sounds good. I'll be back in a few." Travis went out into the sunny parking lot.

"Coming for lunch?" asked Nathaniel.

"Not today. I'm taking your advice, talking to Eli this afternoon. Just grabbing takeout."

"Sounds good." Nathaniel clapped his shoulder. "Praying for you."

Travis jabbed Nathaniel's side with his elbow. "Thanks. Back atcha." He turned away, dialed the Golden Grill, and ordered for him and Eli.

Half an hour later, he pulled back into the parking lot at Creekside Fellowship to see Eli sitting on a planter near the main doors, his thumbs flying over the keyboard on his phone.

Travis couldn't text half that quickly. Didn't get much practice with the limited cell service up at the ranch.

Eli looked up, pocketed his phone, and stood. "Hey. Let's walk."

They crossed the manicured lawn area of the park then found the trail into the wilder part along the creek. "There's my spot." Eli pointed at a large, moss-covered log. "I bring my lunch out here pretty often. Done a bit of counseling out here, too."

Travis parked his backside and opened the bag. He

handed Eli one of the two bottles of pop and the top sandwich before pulling out the second one. He'd never get tired of the Golden Grill's bacon cheeseburgers loaded with onion rings.

"Let's ask the Lord's blessing." Eli bowed his head and launched into prayer.

Travis was in good hands. Eli's… and God's.

"So, talk to me whenever you're ready." Eli took a big bite of his Reuben.

By the time they'd both finished their lunches, Travis had filled Eli in on the short version of his history with Dakota, most of which Eli had figured out over the years. Then he told him what happened Friday, including Dakota's ultimatum.

Eli stared down at the gurgling creek. "I'm not really good at relationships," he said at last. "You may have noticed I'm single."

"It's more the God part I need help with. And the anger part."

"Right." The pastor stretched out his legs and leaned against the log. "The part where you start by forgiving your parents."

Forgiveness again. "Do I have to?"

"No."

Travis laughed. "That's not what I expected you to say."

"Well, it's true. You're an adult. You don't have to do anything. But for every choice we make, whether positive or negative, there's an outcome. You can continue to choose not to forgive them as you've been doing for however many years." Eli angled a look at him. "How's that working for you?"

"Gotcha." Travis snorted. "It landed me right here, on the psychiatrist's couch."

"I'm no shrink, bro. What I've studied is God's word with a minor in human tendencies. But the thing is, we can't keep doing the same thing and expect different results. If you want to change the outcome, my friend, you need to do something different."

"Like forgive them." Travis shifted on the log.

"What have you got to lose?"

Good question. He couldn't think of anything positive that would disappear. He picked up a small stick and broke it into a dozen pieces before releasing a long breath. "Nothing worth keeping."

"What have you got to gain?"

"I dunno. Peace?"

"Peace is worth a lot."

"Even if they don't deserve it."

"None of us deserves forgiveness, Travis. We've all wronged God in more ways than we could ever count. Than we could ever atone for. All we can do is be grateful God doesn't keep score. If we ask Him to forgive us, He wipes the slate clean."

"That's the thing, though. My parents — they haven't asked." Although maybe that's why Monica had come. He hadn't really let her get the words out.

"Is your dad a believer?"

"Declan? No. He sent us to church as kids to get some free time from us. After he married Kathryn, he let her keep bringing us. I've never understood why she married him."

"And your mom?"

"I doubt it, from the language she was spewing at Declan on Friday, but I don't really know her at all. She left sixteen years ago."

Eli nodded. "But you... you're a Christian, right?"

"Yes, sir. I believed as a kid, wandered my own way, and have come back in the past few years. Since Dakota and I split. I knew I needed God to help me be a different kind of father to Toby than what I'd experienced. I couldn't do it by myself."

"Bingo."

Travis waited for Eli to say more, but the only sound was the rushing creek. *"Bingo? That's all you've got to say?"*

Eli laughed. "We can't do any of it on our own. You can't forgive your parents without divine intervention. And you can't overcome your anger without dealing with the root cause."

That made sense. So much sense.

"So, I ask you again, what have you got to gain?"

Everything. The answer was everything.

"I HAVEN'T WAITRESSED IN YEARS."

Estelle Mulligan harrumphed into the phone. "Do you want the job or not? Isobel broke her leg falling off a horse. We need someone to cover her shifts starting in two hours, and for the next six weeks. Sage said you might be available. If not, I need to dig into the file of resumes and start calling people."

Working evenings Wednesday through Sunday wouldn't be so bad. Sage said she'd watch Toby, so that was okay. Dakota would have all day with him until preschool started, then half-days. More time than she'd had while working at From Stetsons to Spurs, actually.

Maybe this was an answer to prayer. She'd certainly never been called out of the blue and offered a job before. "Okay. Let's try it for the six weeks and see how it goes."

"The servers bring in decent tips."

Oh. Dakota hadn't even thought of that. "Sounds good. What time do you need me there?"

"Your shift will be four-thirty to ten-thirty. If you come today at four, I'll get someone to show you around and get you started. Wear black pants and a white top."

"Okay. I'll be there." She hung up from the Golden Grill and called Sage. "Thanks. Now get over here so I can thank you properly."

Sage giggled. "I take it my mom called?"

"She did." Dakota let out all the breath she'd been holding. "Will you really watch Toby? That's a lot of hours."

"I'll come over and bring popcorn." The line went dead.

"Hey, buddy." Dakota looked into Toby's room where he sat on his rug with all his Toy Story action figures around him. "What's up?"

He glowered at her. "I want Daddy."

We can't always have what we want. But she bit the words back before they came out. "I know, buddy. It just didn't work out this weekend."

Which was sort of a lie. She could certainly have let Travis take his son on Friday night, but she wouldn't have slept a wink for worry. He'd also called a couple of times on Saturday, and she'd ignored him. She'd been in Butte, after all. And he might have stopped by after church today. How would she know? She'd accepted an invitation over to Lyssa and Kirk's in Agate Bay just so she wouldn't be home.

She'd held the line for an entire weekend. Big whoop-de-do. Did they give medals for that?

There was a tap at the back door, and she went to let Sage and her huge bowl of popcorn in. "That was fast."

"I have ways." Sage brushed past her. "Hey, Toby, want some popcorn?"

"Yeah!" He came running, always ready for food. Just like his daddy.

"We'll let Mama get a little bowl just for you, okay?"

Toby crossed his arms. "Big bowl."

"A middle-sized bowl." Dakota ruffled his hair, and he scowled as he ducked away.

They all went into the kitchen where she found a mixing bowl and poured it nearly full for Toby. There was still plenty left. He turned away, hugging it against his chest.

"What do you say?"

"Thank you, Miss Sage."

"You're welcome, cowpoke."

He frowned at her. "I Daddy's cowpoke."

"Be nice, Toby."

The scowl got deeper, but Dakota let him get away with it. She sat near Sage on the sofa and helped herself to a handful of buttery, salty goodness.

"Thanks, Sage. Do you really know what you're getting in for with that child?"

"We'll be fine."

"Starting tonight?" Dakota checked her watch and gulped. "In one hour?"

"It's just to help you get back on your feet, sweetie. You'll get things figured out. When Mom told me about Isobel's accident, you just sprang to mind. It seemed to be a God-thing."

"The timing is certainly good, except for you. You'll be coming home from work every day and straight into child-care. I appreciate it. Don't get me wrong. But Toby's not going to be easy. He's never had anyone besides Travis or me tucking him in."

Travis. Her heart hurt at the thought of him. He'd been so angry... but she hadn't given him an inch for explanation, either. Inside her heart, she knew he would never hurt his son.

It was her own heart she was protecting, not Toby's. She'd let herself get caught up in Travis's kisses and gentleness. Somehow, she'd needed to probe to see where the old Travis was. Well, she'd found him, but it didn't make her happy.

Should she have left Toby with Emma like Travis expected? She couldn't have. The teen had vaulted onto her horse and bounded away after listening probably a minute too long to her father's invective. But Dakota could have taken Toby down to Travis's cabin and waited there for at least a little while. She could have left him a note. She could have not hidden on her return to Jewel Lake. She could have accepted his first phone call.

She'd escalated everything until there didn't seem any way to back down, and now she was stuck with it. She'd talk to Travis in a few days, maybe Wednesday at the fairgrounds. Oh, drat. She'd have to miss that. She'd be at the Golden Grill during the kids' practice.

Friday then. Or... there was always the phone, though Travis didn't often have access to cell coverage. Still, she could text him and then accept his call when he phoned her.

But then she remembered the hardness in his gaze when he'd looked through the peephole Friday night.

There was going to be no easy kiss-and-make-up. They could go back to sharing Toby, and she needed to tell him that before he got the law involved. But whatever had been brewing between them? It was gone.

Dakota had killed it. She'd overreacted.

CHAPTER TWENTY-THREE

F ine. I'll pick him up from your place at three-thirty on Wednesday. Have him ready. Please." Travis tapped to end the call while Dakota was still talking.

How magnanimous she sounded. She'd *allow* Toby to spend weekends with his dad as he was accustomed to. She'd *allow* him to go to the fairgrounds on Wednesdays. She wouldn't interfere.

The conversation had started out reasonably enough, but deteriorated rapidly when she hesitated. He'd had to tell her he'd contact an attorney if she didn't relent. She had no grounds for a restraining order.

She'd started to pull a sob story, but when he'd pressed, she'd flipped to the drill sergeant in the blink of an eye. Now *that* was the Dakota he knew and didn't love, but at least he knew how to deal with her that way. Make clear, firm requests and expect her to concede. Which she had done.

Winning didn't feel all that satisfying, but at least he'd see his son. He'd be the best dad he could possibly be for Toby. It had been his mission in life for the past four years. Only a month ago he'd awakened to the hope of more, so he hadn't lost anything. Not really.

Except his heart.

Why did Dakota have to be so stubborn and so infuriating?

"How'd it go, Travis?"

He turned to see Nathaniel and shrugged. "As good as could be expected, I guess. We're back to normal. Whatever that is."

His stepbrother's eyebrows rose. "The old normal or the more recent normal?"

"The old one." Travis pivoted into the stable to saddle up Lancaster.

"Bro, I'm sorry."

"Yeah, well, me, too."

"Did you apologize?"

Travis froze and turned slowly. "She didn't give me a chance. She got all snooty on me in two seconds flat."

"An apology doesn't depend on fertile ground. It's for your sake, regardless of her response."

"Oh, man. I forgot." Travis rubbed the back of his neck. "My habits are set so deep, I just flipped when she did."

"Call her back? You can't give up now."

Watch him.

But his stepbrother was right. Travis had been so hopeful after talking to Eli yesterday. He'd rehearsed how the phone call would go. He'd call her bluff on withholding

Toby — his son was the most important part of the situation, after all — and then he'd apologize for leaving her on Friday and then he'd tell her he forgave her, whether she returned the apology or not. One, two, three, done.

Yeah, that had gone over like half a ton of horseflesh, flying hooves and all.

But... couldn't he have done better? She exasperated him, but he loved her. He'd forgotten how much until the last few weeks. He'd set aside his pride, his sense of rightness, and agreed to her truce. And hadn't it been worth every single minute? Not just the hours where they'd talked like civilized human beings. Not only the times they'd kissed slow and languid, fast and fierce. Not just the moments where Toby had taken them each by the hand, swinging them, and smiling up at first one parent than the other.

Not just all of that.

Dakota was right for him. She might bring out his worst side, but she also brought out his best. He suspected he had the same impact on her. Their magnetism flipped from stubbornly clinging to violently repelling.

But what if they focused on Jesus instead of on Toby? On Jesus instead of each other? Could that forge them into one unit? If Jesus couldn't glue them together, nothing could. Wasn't it worth one solid, final, real attempt?

Travis tipped his hat back and looked Nathaniel in the eye. "You're right. I don't know how to do this, but you're right."

Nathaniel nodded, clouted him on the shoulder, and turned into Kingpin's box stall.

Call her back now, while she was still angry with him? Maybe if he'd calmed down a little, felt some regret, she had, too. Better now than letting it go until he got back from fieldwork late tonight.

He tapped her number. It rang three times and went to voicemail. She wasn't going to make this easy for him. Okay, then.

HE'D ONLY TRIED to call back once more, but Dakota hadn't picked up. Hadn't he said everything there was to say? Cross him again and there'd be a lawyer involved. He was Toby's father, he had rights, blah blah blah. Why pick up another call like a desperate woman and listen to more of the same?

None of it was wrong. He'd overreacted. She'd overreacted. Now they were back in that crazy hostile environment where they'd spent the majority of Toby's life. They were both at fault.

Lord, I don't know what to do.

Sage was in the smug I-knew-it-wouldn't-work camp. Mom was there, too. But were they the best judges? Possibly not.

God was a God of forgiveness. Of second chances. Like the father of the prodigal son, He welcomed people back with open arms and a celebration.

If Dakota was going to take anyone's example, it should be God's. Not Sage's. Not Mom's. Sage had never said why she refused to talk to Caleb for something like a decade. She could hold a grudge like nobody's business. Mom had become a mouse who accepted everything Dad doled out without a squeak. She could turn the other cheek like no one else Dakota knew… with the possible exception of Travis's stepmother, Kathryn.

But wasn't there a happy medium? A place where mutual forgiveness happened along with mutual respect between two people who kept their eyes focused on Jesus first?

She'd caught Travis out on his front porch at dawn, reading his Bible on an app. He talked comfortably about what he'd been reading. He took Toby to church every week. He prayed over meals, not a rote grace, but personal words of gratitude.

Maybe Travis was really trying. Not to impress Dakota, but because he felt the need for a right relationship with God deep inside himself.

Of course, just a few minutes ago, he'd hung up on her. He did have a temper, but she could appreciate that he'd rather avoid the confrontation than blast ugly words at her like both their fathers had the habit of doing.

They should try another truce. Dakota chewed on her lip and stared at her phone for a long minute or two before picking it up and tapping his number. It went to voicemail. Of course, it did. If he'd moved thirty feet away from the house or stable, he had no coverage. By the time he got in from whatever today's task was, she'd be at the Golden Grill.

It would have to wait until Wednesday afternoon. They'd have a brief window of time when he came for Toby before she had to be at work. Of course, that meant his twin sisters would be eagerly listening and watching, but it couldn't be helped. A message on his voicemail wouldn't do the trick.

TRAVIS GROWLED IN FRUSTRATION. The notification on his phone showed Dakota had called not long after he'd hung up on her this morning. Of course, she hadn't left a message. Now, when he returned the call, he was the one shuttled to voicemail. He wasn't inclined to leave a message, either.

This was stupidly ridiculous. Dakota didn't have a job anymore, but it seemed she was too busy to talk to him, regardless. Maybe she was out with — no. She'd told him that had been a sham to make him jealous. It had worked.

He hadn't even asked her what had happened at the western shop. He hadn't even asked her if that's why she'd pulled Toby from daycare. He hadn't even asked about her job search, what she was going to do now, how she was going to pay rent without income.

No, it had all been about him and his reaction to the exposure of his childhood wounds.

Was that how a man loved a woman?

The airhorn blasted for dinner. Travis washed up in the stable's restroom and crossed the yard as his brothers gathered from around the ranch.

"Get the irrigation lines moved?" Blake asked Ryder.

The youngest Cavanagh nodded. "Trav, the pump's got a funny sound, though. Can you check on that?"

Most mechanical stuff was up to Travis. They only called in a mechanic from John Deere in Missoula if he couldn't figure it out. "I'll have a look at it in the morning."

"Alexia mentioned Destiny has a limp."

"That'll be up to Noah. When is he home?"

"Thursday," answered Nathaniel. "He'll be here for a couple of days to reshoe all the horses."

The guys moved into the dining room. Declan appointed Nathaniel to ask the blessing then Cook served up a pot roast loaded with vegetables and mentioned there was pie for dessert.

Travis took a heaping plateful. Hard work in the mountain air gave a guy plenty of appetite. It sure was nice not to have to think about cooking for himself at the end of a long day.

A sneak glance at Riley made him wonder, though. Adam was home from the hospital but not up to making the trek to the main house for a big meal. He was still on soft foods, and Riley would take whatever Cook had prepared back to him.

Travis knew Riley and Adam were biding their time in hopes of moving down to the house at Running Creek, which Kathryn had, for some reason, deeded to Declan upon their marriage. It was the ranch next door, where Adam and his brothers had spent their younger years.

Dakota wouldn't likely be as patient as Riley... if she'd ever allow Travis to make things up to her.

He couldn't wait until Wednesday to see her, and it wasn't like they could really talk at the fairgrounds, either. It was a social gathering for the parents of horse-loving kids, and he needed to be paying attention in case Toby, Alexia, or Emma needed him.

What they really needed was a date night, one without their son. Was there any way Dakota would agree? They could go for a drive or a ride or something where they could talk uninterrupted if he brought one or both of the twins to babysit. Dakota used to love to ride. Since she wasn't working, maybe she'd be willing to go out one evening this week.

If she'd ever talk to him again.

He sopped up the last of his gravy with a slice of sourdough bread, pushed his plate aside, and looked around the table. His twin sisters had been uncharacteristically quiet since Friday. Sullen, even.

Kathryn's spot was vacant. As far as Travis knew, she hadn't come out of her basement suite since Monica's visit. His stepmother was another person Travis needed to apologize to. The list was lengthening. She'd done her best with the three wild colts that had come with her marriage to Declan. It wasn't her fault Travis had rejected her. He'd been angry with his own mother and taken it out on her.

But first, Dakota. Then Kathryn. Then Noah, the last of the stepbrothers he hadn't reconciled with. Probably wouldn't hurt to talk to his own younger brothers, too.

Man, he had a heap of sensitivity coming up. He needed to get started on it. Why didn't he just drive down to Jewel Lake right after pie and confront Dakota in person? No, not confront. That was the old Travis. The new Travis would arrive humbly, quietly, repentantly. It wasn't going to come easy, but with God's help, he'd do it. It would be worth it.

Cook served out gigantic slices of steaming huckleberry pie with vanilla ice cream on top. Travis shoveled it in, thinking of his drive down the mountain.

"So, about your mother…" Declan cleared his throat and looked between his sons.

And all Travis's thoughts and plans went out the window.

CHAPTER TWENTY-FOUR

This was so far from ideal, but one of the servers had called in sick, and Dakota could get a couple of extra hours. Mom was free to watch Toby at the duplex until Travis picked him up. And Sage would be there by the time Travis brought him back.

It would be perfect if she still wanted to avoid Travis at all costs. In fact, that's what it would look like to him. She knew it, but what could she do about it?

She could leave him a message.

But so could he, and he hadn't. He'd called a couple of other times, never catching her. She'd tried him once... and missed. How could he stand living up the mountain with such lousy connectivity?

She'd asked him that once, years ago when they were together. Back then, they didn't even have cell service at all. Everything was on a landline in the house, shop, or stable. They'd boosted in basic cell service since, but the area it covered was minimal. Probably the signal had been meant to improve internet for the twins' schooling.

Either way, Travis's and her lame attempts to contact each other in the past couple of days had utterly failed. To be fair, she was a bit leery and didn't try that hard, because she couldn't be sure which Travis she was going to get. She'd counted on figuring that out in the five minutes she saw him while he picked up their son. If he sent in one of the twins or sat at the curb and honked, that would tell her everything she needed to know.

She grabbed her purse and bent to give Toby a kiss. "Be good for Grandma and Daddy."

He looked at her with suspicion. "Daddy coming, right?"

"In one hour. Promise." Travis better not make her eat those words.

"Come on, little man. Let's bake some cookies." Mom stretched her hand toward Toby.

"And *you* be nice to Travis, too."

"Of course." Mom smiled a little too brightly.

Oh, boy. Not that Dakota had a lot of options if she wanted to make rent at the end of the month, and she definitely did.

All through her shift, she kept an eye on the clock. Travis should be coming for Toby about now. Toby would be on Clover, grinning from ear to ear as he rode the barrels about now. Now Travis would be dropping him off for Sage, and Toby would be clinging to his daddy. Hopefully Sage would be patient with him. She'd stopped by for takeout on her way home from work, but Estelle handled that. The diner had been too busy for Dakota to take a minute.

Now Sage would be giving Toby a bath then reading

him a story from her Beatrix Potter collection, while Toby pouted that he wanted a cowboy story instead. Dakota really, really missed tucking her little boy in bed every night, and this was only the fourth evening.

It was eight o'clock when Estelle hurried over to her with worry on her face. "Sage is on the phone for you."

It was against the rules to take private calls at the diner. Dakota's phone was tucked in her purse. "I — is it okay for me to talk to her?"

Estelle nodded abruptly. "Take a break. Answer."

"Okay." Dakota gave her boss a sidelong look and went to the diner's phone on the counter. "Hello?"

"Dakota?"

"Yes?"

Sage hiccupped. "I don't know how to tell you this, but Toby's gone."

Dakota froze. "What do you mean, *gone*?"

"I mean I tucked him in bed and now he's not there and his shoes are gone and so is Woody and he must have gone out the backdoor because I can't find him anywhere and I'm *freaking out*."

A clamp tightened around Dakota's head and another around her heart. Travis? But if he were going to take Toby from her, he wouldn't have brought him back from the fairgrounds.

Her other hand was already fumbling for the apron ties. "I'm coming." She dropped the phone to its cradle and turned to Estelle. "Toby's missing. I'm leaving."

The woman shooed her toward the door. "I will pray. If you need anything else, let me know."

So different from Pete. "Thanks."

Dakota dashed out the backdoor, jumped in her car, and sped home. It wasn't far, but even though Jewel Lake was a smallish town, it was just off the interstate, and she didn't feel safe walking alone after dark. Right now, she was thankful for the speed, but she kept an eye out for a little boy clutching a plush cowboy while she drove.

She whipped out at home and dashed in the door. "Have you found him yet?"

"No." Sage wrung her hands while tears dribbled down her face. "I'm so sorry, Dakota. I don't know what I'll do if he—"

Dakota sliced her hand, cutting off her friend's lament. There was no *if*. They'd find Toby, and they'd find him quickly. Anything else was absolutely unthinkable. She charged into Toby's room, looked under his bed. In his closet. In her room, the same. The bathroom. Behind the couch. Sage was right. Toby wasn't in the townhouse. Small comfort he had Woody with him. And his backpack.

She yanked her phone out of her purse and tapped Travis's number.

Straight to voicemail. Here they went again. She growled in frustration. Why did the man even own a cellphone? Then she hunted down the Rockstead Ranch house number and punched it in. *Come on, come on. Someone pick up.*

It took two rings. "Rockstead," said a guy's voice.

"I need Travis. Right away."

"Uh, he's not in the house. Who's calling? I'll get him to call you back."

"It's Dakota. I need him immediately. Toby's missing."

There was no time to curl up and panic. Not when her baby was out there with night soon falling.

SOMEONE POUNDED on his door then flung it open before Travis had taken two steps toward it. He reared back. "Ryder? What's up?"

"Dakota just phoned the house. She says Toby's missing. Call her."

"No way!" Travis staggered back. "Is this for real?"

"Sure sounded like it to me."

He'd planned to drive down to Jewel Lake last night before Declan's little discussion after supper. Then it seemed too late, knowing Toby would be in bed soon. Not that this trip or discussion was to see his son, but it didn't seem fair to spring a visit on Dakota right then without warning.

Okay, he'd chickened out, but Declan had given him a lot to think about. His mind was racing. Divided. But Dakota and Toby came first. They had to. Every single time.

And today her mother had been at the duplex and refused to explain where Dakota was. Everyone was against them.

Travis grabbed his cowboy hat off the rack by the door. "What else did she say?"

"That's it."

"Okay then. Thanks."

"Want me to come with you?" Ryder jogged to keep up while Travis strode down the cabin steps.

"Uh… that would be a good idea, so long as someone knows where we've gone. Did you tell anyone else?"

"Not yet. I came straight for you."

"Then spread the word. Ask everyone to pray. And then you and whoever can, drive on down so we can cover more ground looking for him." He flung his truck door open and jumped in. "Got it?"

"Yes, sir."

Any other time, and Travis would have laughed at his little brother's response. Not today. He jammed the key in the ignition and roared out of the ranch yard. Who cared how much dust he stirred up? His son was missing. His pride and joy.

Too late, he remembered he hadn't called Dakota back, and now he was out of cell service again. He would be until he hit the highway near Jewel Lake. Well, it couldn't be helped now. He wasn't wasting the time needed to drive back to the ranch yard and make a phone call.

Sage called Lyssa. Lyssa called Pastor Eli. Pastor Eli phoned a few others. Before Dakota knew it, a dozen people were gathered in her townhouse while Eli organized them into search teams. She texted a recent photo of Toby to every number offered her.

None of the people in her townhouse was Travis Cavanagh. Nor had he phoned, despite Ryder's promise he would.

The group scattered.

"Someone needs to stay here and coordinate things. Do you want me to do that?"

Dakota turned to her mother on wooden limbs. "I don't know. Maybe I should be the one? *I don't know*!" She'd been holding it together for over half an hour, but now the dam burst and the tears erupted. She sagged into her mother's arms. "How could this have happened? I need my baby!"

Dad stood there, awkwardly frowning.

A truck roared up and the engine cut out.

"Grand entrance for the reprobate," mumbled Dad.

Dakota shot to the door and flung it open as Travis launched out of his vehicle toward her. Any fleeting thought he might be responsible for Toby's disappearance fled at the sense of determined purpose he exuded as he strode toward her.

No thought needed. She stepped into his arms and crushed him as tightly as he crushed her.

"Tell me everything." His hands tightened on her back.

"Sage called me at work—"

"Back up. What work? Why Sage? Your mother said nothing when I picked up Toby this afternoon, just sent him out to the truck."

Didn't that just figure? And Sage had probably been just as helpful afterward.

"I've been working evenings at the diner since Sunday. I needed a job, Travis, and it's been all I could find so far. Sage watches him and puts him to bed. It's not ideal, but I didn't know what else to do." She heard the panic rising in her voice but felt helpless to stop it.

"More on that later," Travis said gruffly. "And tonight?"

"She called me at eight. She'd tucked him in bed, but

when she checked to see if he'd fallen asleep half an hour later, he wasn't there. He's got his backpack and Woody, and he's definitely nowhere in the house. I've checked under beds, in closets, everywhere."

Travis squeezed her. "We need a search party. My brothers are coming. All except Adam. He's still stuck in bed, but he's praying."

He'd referred to Adam as his brother? The Lord really had been doing some miracles.

"There's already a search party. Lyssa and Kirk, Sage, Eli, a bunch of people from your church that I don't even know. They just left a few minutes ago."

"Okay. Good. The police?"

She choked back a sob. "I should call them, I guess."

"I'll do it in a minute. Where could he have gone?"

"If I knew, I'd have found him already."

"Good point." His arms tightened around her so much she couldn't even breathe. "Dakota, it's not your fault. You hear me? It's not. You've done everything you could."

How could he know the guilt she felt? She soaked his shirt with her tears.

"Toby's got a good head on his shoulders. It'll be okay, sweetheart. I love you."

She'd been longing for those words all week, and they were more precious than ever. But they couldn't stem the tears. How could she and Travis get past this if — no. She wasn't going there. Not at all. Her baby had been gone less than an hour, total. It was July. Not too cold. She wouldn't think about their proximity to the interstate or the creek a few blocks away or anything like that.

Please, Jesus, keep my baby safe and bring him home.

She'd prayed that a thousand times already, and if she had to beg a thousand more times, she'd do it.

Travis kissed her hair then released her.

She staggered a little and pressed her hands to her eyes, trying to wipe them dry.

He phoned the state troopers and, with a crisp, emotionless voice, gave the bare details.

The lack of emotion wasn't from lack of caring. Dakota knew that now. It was because he could compartmentalize and think under pressure, not fall apart like she did.

"Now come inside and sit down, sweetheart. The cops are on their way over, and then we'll join the search party if he's not found yet. God's got this." Travis held her hands between them. "Father God, we bring our son before You and ask You to watch over him and bring him safely home. He's only a little guy, God, and he needs his mama and daddy." Now his voice choked.

"Amen," whispered Dakota, and threw herself back into Travis's strong arms.

CHAPTER TWENTY-FIVE

W e'll find him." Declan's voice brooked no argument. His piercing eyes and unyielding tone must have made all six boys cringe into obedience as kids.

Dakota might not love Travis's father, but she could grab onto his absolute determination. He said he'd stop at nothing, and she believed him.

Declan gestured at his other three sons — Blake, Ryder, and Nathaniel — and the men strode out, climbed into two black Rockstead Ranch trucks just like Travis's, and drove away to the area along Creekside Park where the police sergeant had sent them.

Dakota couldn't bear thinking about Toby near that tumbling body of water. He wouldn't have walked that far, would he? But where was he? She turned to Travis, who gathered her tight once more.

"They've got Jewel Lake covered, but is there anywhere nearby? He wouldn't have gone over to Sage's, would he?"

She shook her head. "Sage keeps her doors locked

whether she's inside or not. He couldn't get in, even if he wanted to." And Dakota was pretty sure Toby wouldn't have wanted to. He'd been okay with Sage as a neighbor but hadn't exactly warmed to her as a caregiver.

"You kids go look if you want." Mom waved toward the door. "We can hold down the fort."

"Are you sure?"

Dad draped his arm over Mom's shoulder. "Yeah, sure."

"Does he like the playground?" asked Travis.

"He does, but they've already checked it."

Travis shrugged. "Toby's mobile. There's no reason to think he's in the same place he was an hour ago."

That was supposed to be an encouragement? Because it wasn't. Still, she was going to go berserk stuck in the house with her parents, even if Dad seemed like he cared for once. She needed to actually help in the search. "Okay. Let's look."

Travis took her hand and ushered her out. They walked the shortcut toward where she'd parked the other day, calling Toby's name.

"You looking for the little guy?" A neighbor in sweat shorts and a baggy, not-so-white undershirt asked over the fence.

Dakota pivoted. "Yes, have you seen him?"

"Not today, no. Cute little gaffer."

"If you spot him, let the police know, please. He's been gone over an hour, and we have search parties out all over town." She tried to squash her panic at the angle of the sun. It wasn't long until it would dip over the lake and leave the town in darkness.

"I'm sure sorry to hear that. I'll keep my eye out."

"Thanks."

"Appreciated," put in Travis, pulling her back to walking. "You've got a great neighborhood here."

"I know." She sniffled. "Trav, I'm so sorry. About everything."

His hand tightened on her upper arm and pulled her close against his side. "You can't be half as sorry as I am, sweetheart. I've let you and Toby down so many times. It kills me." His voice broke.

"Oh, Travis." She turned toward him and wrapped her arms around his waist, clutching him tight. "What will we do if—"

"Shh." He kissed her hair. "Don't go there. We'll find him."

"But what if we don't?"

"We will."

His blind refusal to see the possibility of failure should irritate her more than it did. If only she could cling to faith like he did. His belief was real, not delusion.

"Travis, I've been guilty of lumping you in with my dad and yours. Temper. Anger. I haven't allowed myself to believe you could be different…"

"Because I'm not different. I'm my father's son."

She shook her head against his chest. "You're so, so different."

"How do you see that? His temper is always lurking just beneath the surface." His hands tightened. "So's mine."

"But he doesn't seem to care if he explodes and who's around to see it when he does. Like Friday."

"I wasn't any better. I—"

"You were a thousand times better. I'm sorry I couldn't see it at first. I saw what I expected to see, but—"

"Point proved."

"No, not at all. Your father got in your mother's face and yelled obscenities at her with no regard for witnesses. Toby. Emma. Me. Nathaniel. No one mattered to him in the face of his fury."

"Uh huh."

"But you wouldn't allow us to see your rage. You didn't try to pretend it didn't exist. You separated yourself from the situation and dealt with it elsewhere. I bet you talked to God about it."

"If you can call bellowing *why?* at Him while heaving rocks into the creek, sure."

Dakota's heart settled as she tilted her head back to look at him. "That's exactly what I mean."

His brows furrowed beneath the brim of his cowboy hat. "I don't get it."

"Is Declan asking God to help him make sense of it?"

"Not so much."

"But you are. All I could see in that moment was how angry you were and how you abandoned Toby and me." She gulped in air. "Memories came back."

He looked away, his jaw tensing, but Dakota cradled his stubbled cheeks between her hands until he looked back.

"But, Travis... you weren't abandoning us. You were protecting us. You were dealing with what you saw as the biggest threat first. I didn't see it. I'm sorry. I get it now." Now that it might be too late.

"Seeing Monica... that just shocked me to the core. I went cold inside at the thought of her knowing about

Toby, but I knew you wouldn't let anything happen to him."

A new fear struck Dakota. "Monica... she couldn't be behind this, could she?"

Travis shook his head. "I really don't think so, but I'll mention it to the police when we get back to the house. He crushed Dakota tight against his chest. "It will be okay, sweetheart. It *will*." And he launched into a heartfelt prayer for the safety of their son and the success of the searchers.

The last bit of reluctance melted away as Dakota echoed his words through tears of her own.

His ARM still tight around Dakota, Travis surveyed the open area. There was a set of swings, a row of teeter-totters, several slides of varying heights, and a jungle gym with assorted ways to climb and swing, all in an area grounded with shredded tires. Around the area sat a few park benches and one open picnic shelter with a couple of tables in it. A paved walkway ran the perimeter. It would be great for kids on bikes or skateboards. "There's no place to hide in this playground."

"I know. It's one reason I like it so much."

"I can see that." Though right now, Travis only wished for a thousand hidey-holes so that one of them might contain his son. He turned slowly, scanning the area, then letting his gaze swing further out to include the streets that spoked out from the park.

Where was his little boy wearing cowboy pajamas and a

Toy Story backpack and clutching a plush Woody under his arm? *Lord Jesus, where is he?*

A black truck rolled by, and Travis took a step toward it before realizing it didn't have the Rockstead Ranch emblem on the door. The driver wasn't one of his brothers.

"That guy just moved into the unit behind us. His truck keeps catching me off-guard, too. Once Toby talked about how you didn't stop and see him."

Travis narrowed his gaze at the vehicle as it turned the corner. "So, Toby didn't notice it didn't have our logo?"

Dakota looked up at him, frowning. "I mentioned it once, but he still got confused after that."

"Does he drive by often?"

"All the time, like he's paid to do it. Wait. What are you thinking?"

He grabbed her hand and started running toward the truck with its taillights disappearing around the corner. "Let's go meet your neighbor."

The truck was the same make and model as Travis's. A little spark of pride flared in his heart that his four-year-old could recognize his daddy's truck so clearly. It sat parked in front of a townhouse with lights shining from the windows. Someone crossed in front of one of them.

Still pulling Dakota, Travis marched up the front walk and rang the doorbell.

A thickset guy with a cowboy hat answered the door, looking between Travis and Dakota. "Whatever you're selling, I'm not buying."

Travis put his boot in the door before it closed. "Just a sec. Please. Your truck is just like mine."

"So? I bought it fair and square."

"That's not what I meant. Look, my little boy keeps thinking it's you driving by the duplex right behind here. He went missing tonight, and we're wondering if he saw your truck and followed it. He… he's been missing me."

"Aw, a little kid is out there, lost? Why didn't you say so? What does he look like?"

Dakota pulled her phone out of her pocket and turned Toby's picture toward the man. "He's only four, and it's been an hour and a half already. We're so worried."

The man stroked his jaw. "You've called the police?"

"We have." Travis's fingers tangled with Dakota's again as soon as she'd put her phone away. "There are dozens of people out searching for him. I know it's a long shot, but have you seen him tonight?"

"Might've. Couple of hours ago I headed out toward Agate Bay and saw some movement in that backyard over there." He pointed toward Dakota's. "Little gaffer like that, hope he's okay."

"Which route did you take to the highway?"

The man explained.

"Thanks. Gives us something to check on, anyway." Travis pulled Dakota toward the shortcut through the complex.

"Let me know when he's found!" the guy called.

Dakota waved as they broke into a run. They jumped into Travis's truck, rolled both windows down, and slowly followed the route, calling Toby's name.

As they turned the second corner, Travis's heart began to sink. This was a considerable distance for Toby to go. Was it a testament to how much the boy longed for his daddy, or was this hunch completely off-base?

Travis wasn't letting go once Toby was safe in his arms. Never again.

The screeching whine of a saw cutting metal ripped the air. "Yeeow. That's unexpected and loud."

"Stop the truck."

Travis veered to the curb and hit the brakes. "Do you see something?"

"No. But Toby hates loud noises. I wonder how long that person has been working out there."

But Travis was already out of the truck and running past the house to the workshop in back. Now someone was pounding metal with a sledgehammer.

Toby would definitely not approve.

A quick exchange with the metalworker confirmed he'd been at it for hours, trying to get his project completed before daylight faded completely. He hadn't seen a little kid, but that was no surprise.

Travis returned to the truck. Dakota was halfway down the block back toward her place, calling Toby's name.

"Hey, baby, Mama's here. So is Daddy. Where are you, Toby?"

And before Travis's very eyes, a little figure in green pajamas and a navy backpack darted out from beneath a bush and flung himself into his mama's waiting arms.

Travis could've won Olympic gold for his sprint to his family's side. He scooped both Dakota and Toby into his arms and twirled them around before setting them back to the sidewalk.

Dakota smothered Toby's face with kisses in between sobs.

Toby patted his mother's cheek, tears flowing down his face, as well. And then he reached for Travis.

Travis didn't have the heart to take the boy from Dakota. He gathered them together and wrapped his arms around them both.

His family. They'd never be apart again.

CHAPTER TWENTY-SIX

I can't believe you're letting him stay again." Mom gave a disapproving sniff in the direction of the living room where Travis lay sound asleep on the sofa with Toby sprawled across his chest, safe in his daddy's arms. "What will people think?"

"Maybe they'll think that Toby needed his daddy and that I didn't have the heart to separate them."

There'd been far too much excitement when they returned to the townhouse. Travis had called off the search, and dozens of people had stopped by to see Toby for themselves. There'd been a police report to sign off and, by the time nearly everyone was gone, it was almost midnight.

Declan had reached for the doorknob but now turned back. "Mind your own business, Maude. Our kids are adults. They can do what they want."

"Of course, *you'd* say that," Mom shot back. "You don't have any morals to speak of."

"You're wrong. Don't you dare interfere with my grandson, you hear me?"

Mom rolled her eyes, but she reached for her purse.

Huh. Declan had participated in the entire search. He'd sent Ryder back to the ranch with Blake and Nathaniel after Toby'd been found. Maybe the brusque man did care about Toby and the rest of his family. Dakota had certainly seen a new side of him tonight.

She followed him to the door. "Declan? I can't thank you enough for dropping everything and coming to join the search. It means the world to me."

He searched her face. "I love that kid."

Had he ever told anyone he loved them before? Maybe Monica or Kathryn once or twice. "People need to hear that sometimes."

Declan chuckled sardonically, tipped his hat, and went through the door. "Tell Travis we'll do without him tomorrow."

"I will." She watched him stride out to his black truck.

"What an odious man," Mom said from behind her.

"You know, I don't think he's all that bad, after all. He just... cares, passionately."

"Certainly has a strange way of showing it."

Hard to argue with that. Dakota hugged her mother. "Thanks for sticking around when Dad went home. Looks like Scotty's here to pick you up." Her brother had been in Missoula and missed the search. He might be a lazy bum, but he'd surely have helped if he'd been in town. Dakota would hold onto that thought. She'd had enough of thinking the worst of people.

When her mom finally closed the door behind her,

Dakota turned off the kitchen light and stood in the living room doorway for a long moment watching her guys sleep.

Hadn't Travis proved to her over and over lately how much he loved her and their son? Her heart was full as she reached for a quilt and draped it over the two of them. She leaned down to brush a kiss over Travis's forehead.

An arm snaked out from beneath the quilt and pulled her tight. Travis's head angled just enough that his lips caught hers.

The surprise and passion combined to weaken her legs. She crumpled to kneel beside him, showering kisses on his precious face.

Toby stirred.

"Let me tuck him in," she whispered.

"So long as he doesn't wake up," Travis whispered back. "Because we need to talk."

And kiss.

But she'd moved a sleeping little boy many times before, and she managed without him coming completely awake. Then she returned to the living room where Travis folded the quilt.

He sat down and patted the sofa next to him, and she gladly nestled in. "I know we talked about this a little an hour or two ago, but we've got less on our minds now that our boy is asleep in his own bed."

"And I bolted the backdoor."

"He's not going anywhere." Travis chuckled but then grew serious. "And, Dakota, neither am I. I love you. I love Toby. And I want nothing more than to marry you and make us a real family. We both know I'm not perfect. Even Toby has figured that out. I've got a temper. I've got issues, but God's got my heart, and I promise I'll keep talking to Eli and let God make me more like Him."

"I love you, Travis. I haven't been trying to mend things between us, either."

"You called the truce." His fingers traced her jawline. "That was a huge step. Snapped me out of my funk."

"It was for Toby's sake. And honestly, that kind of worries me."

Travis cupped her cheek with one hand. "How's that?"

"My parents stayed together for Scotty and me. They treat each other terribly."

"I haven't had the best example, either. Well, you know. You've seen it. But we don't have to be like our parents. We've got Jesus on our side, and as long as we keep our eyes focused on Him, I think we'll do okay."

"I can't believe your church just jumped in and helped look for Toby."

"They know him. Love him. But honestly, they're just that kind of people."

"Maybe I'll go to church there on Sunday."

"I never want to be apart from you again."

Dakota looked into Travis's dark eyes, alight with passion. "That could be arranged."

"Will you marry me?"

"Tomorrow." She brushed her lips across his but pulled back before he could capture them. "All we need is a marriage license and someone to perform it."

"There's no waiting time in Montana..." He tugged her closer. "I'd be up for that, no problem, but don't you want a real wedding with all the trimmings? The fancy dress, the flowers, all that?"

"I'm pretty sure I fit my mom's gown. I used to dress up in it when I was a kid and even a teen. And flowers? We can figure something out."

He held her face between his hands, just a breath away. "Are you sure? Because I'd like nothing more. It kills me to be apart from Toby, and even more, to be apart from you. I love you, Dakota. I've never stopped."

"Maybe tomorrow is too soon. How about Saturday? And I'm one-hundred percent certain. I've never stopped loving you, either, and Toby... he needs us both. Together."

"Saturday? Let me call Pastor Marshall." He reached for his phone.

"Travis, it's eleven-thirty! You can't wake the poor man up."

"I guess it can wait until morning." Travis tugged her into his lap. "I heard Declan say I didn't have to work tomorrow, but I also heard your mother, and she's right. It's dangerous for me to stay here."

"I thought you were out for the night."

He grinned and nuzzled her neck. "Nah. I was tired of listening to all of them yammer on. I figured the fewer people responding to every word, the sooner they'd go away."

Dakota giggled. "You were right about that."

"Besides, if we really are getting married on Saturday, I think I can wait that long. I might actually need some sleep, because I'll be back first thing in the morning to go get that marriage license and talk to Pastor Marshall. And then we'll go ring shopping, okay?"

She kissed him lightly. "Sounds good. So long as I'm back by four to go to work."

"You want to keep working at the Golden Grill?"

"I promised Estelle six weeks, and I've only put in one."

"Wow, that sure cuts into my plans. Can you at least get out of Saturday night? Because I'd hate to have to spend the evening without my bride."

"I can ask."

"And after that?"

"Need you ask?" She kissed him.

When they came up for air, he chuckled. "I like that answer, but that wasn't my question. "I don't know where we'll live. I want to talk to Declan about building a house down nearer the highway, but I didn't realize I needed to be in a hurry."

"You can always move in here for now. It's only half an hour up to the ranch. Lots of people have a longer commute."

"I like the way you think, sweetheart. We'll work it all out. Bit by bit."

"Together."

"Always together." He covered her mouth with his and offered her a taste of how beautiful together could be.

DECLAN'S EYEBROWS SHOT UP. "Didn't expect you here for breakfast."

Travis looked his father in the eye. "I didn't want to overstay my welcome at Dakota's. Mrs. Erickson's right. No one needed to wonder what I was doing there all night."

"Like the two of you don't already have a child together."

"Things are different this time around." Travis glanced around the ranch house foyer. Good. All his brothers were present, even Noah. Adam stood with Riley. "We're getting married on Saturday."

"Congrats!" Blake slugged his shoulder. "I get to stand up for you, right?"

"Which Saturday?" Declan's eyes narrowed.

"In two days. That one."

"Whoa, dude," muttered Ryder.

Declan stepped closer. "You're serious?"

"Absolutely. It's not like we don't know each other." One of his brothers snickered, but Travis didn't care which one. "We're in it for the long haul. Not just for Toby's sake, but for any future kids we might have." He'd spent much of his life as one of eight. It hadn't been so bad.

"Congratulations, Travis." Kathryn spoke from the dining room doorway. "I'll pray God blesses your marriage."

Travis nearly felt guilty, but he couldn't fix Kathryn's relationship with his father. They had to do that themselves, and he wasn't sure Declan was willing. Yet, for some reason, they still put on some sort of illusion of it.

His only responsibility was to Dakota. Just because his dad didn't put his wife first — after God — didn't mean Travis had to be just like him. He could break away with God's help. He could set a new course and be an example Toby could follow in years to come.

Then his brothers gave him tight man-hugs, one at a time, with Adam last. "Dude. You've come a long way."

"God's grace, bro. Full of second chances."

Adam grinned. "It's a pretty amazing thing, huh?" His fingers twined with Riley's. "Where you guys gonna live?"

Travis lowered his voice. "In town, for now. I'm gonna talk to Declan — Dad — though. We need to make some changes around here and make things more family friendly. What do you say?"

"I'm in, man. All in." Adam looked down at Riley. "We'd like to start a family, but with everything up in the air about the future of Running Creek, it's hard to know if it's a good time or not."

"I'm headed into town right after breakfast. Have a marriage license to get, some rings to buy. But I'll be back up here this evening with Toby. Get the guys together, and let's come up with a plan. Something all six of us can get behind."

Adam tilted his head. "Tonight? You're not gonna be too busy?"

"Dakota's got to work. It's fine. It's amazing how little there is to prepare for a wedding when you only give it a couple of days."

"Men." Riley laughed. "You have no idea. I'll give Dakota a call while you're driving and see what I can do to help."

Alexia stuck her head out of the dining room. "Are you guys coming in for breakfast or not? I'm kind of starving."

EPILOGUE

S econd chances were a thing.

The thought brought comfort to Nathaniel Cavanagh as he ushered his mother to the front row in Creekside Fellowship, his stepfather trailing behind. This made something like the third time Declan had been in church in the past year. Maybe words Pastor Marshall said today would stick in the man's ears and show him how to be a better husband and father. Every time Nathaniel felt a little hope it was happening, Declan squashed it the next day.

But, hey, Travis and Dakota had managed to wade through a messy, volatile relationship to forgive each other and pledge their lives together. If they could do it, so could Declan and Mom... if they cared enough to try.

And maybe, just maybe, someday Nathaniel would find out why Ainsley Johnson had loved him and ghosted him all in twenty-four hours. He couldn't fix things if he couldn't find her.

Nathaniel took his place in the long line of brothers

with Scotty Erickson at the end. Then little Toby strutted toward the front carrying a ring pillow. On Dakota's side of the platform stood Riley with Sage Mulligan and Lyssa Kennedy. There simply weren't enough women to match up with all these Cavanagh cowboys.

Maybe someday there would be a match for each brother. Nathaniel let his mind go there for a brief moment.

Let himself see Ainsley walking toward him the way Dakota came down the center aisle, her smile radiant and fixed on Travis. A quick glance at Travis revealed an uncharacteristically soft smile with very characteristic focus, including a tic in his jaw as he waited for his bride.

After rough teen years and on into adulthood, Nathaniel had finally come to appreciate this particular stepbrother of his. Blake, closer to his age, and Ryder, the youngest, had included the Anderson twins more readily. Adam had been the victim of most of Travis's hatred, yet here they were, all standing up for Travis, a united front.

If only Ainsley...

Nathaniel swallowed his grief and blinked the tears away. It had been over a year since she'd disappeared from his life after a night that shouldn't have happened. He'd had no clue she'd get cold feet in the blink of an eye.

He'd called the police, for the fat lot of good that had done. Adults were allowed to vanish if they wanted. There'd been no accident. No hospital entry. How could she simply have disappeared?

It was hard to stand here and smile as though nothing was wrong, but then his gaze caught on Travis picking up his young son. Toby put his hands on Travis's and Dakota's as they exchanged vows.

Nathaniel could be happy for them. He could.

But could he ever get past Ainsley and find love for himself?

A NOTE FROM VALERIE:

Aw, don't you feel Nathaniel's agony? He's already tried so hard to find Ainsley, the love of his life. How could he possibly do more? And even if he did locate her... is he ready for what he finds?

Read Nathaniel and Ainsley's story in *Let Me Off Easy, Cowboy*, the third Cavanagh Cowboys Romance.

Did you miss Adam and Riley's story? You'll find it in the first Cavanagh Cowboys Romance, *Marry Me for Real, Cowboy*!

ACKNOWLEDGMENTS

Ah, cowboys! There's just something about them, isn't there? Masculine, hardworking, resourceful, honorable, and gentlemanly... a cowboy is hard to beat.

Thank YOU, dear reader, for loving the Saddle Springs Romance series so much I was inspired to write the Cavanagh Cowboys Romance series as a spin-off. I hope you enjoy the ride. Pun intended!

Always, always, thanks to my fellow author and friend, Elizabeth Maddrey. She prods, cheers, and commiserates as needed, then offers helpful brainstorming and critiques. If you haven't read her Christian contemporary romances, go find them and get started!

I also appreciate my beta readers. Paula and Amy combed through an early draft of *Give Me Another Chance, Cowboy* to find any errors or inconsistencies. I am forever grateful!

My amazing editor, Nicole, has been with me from the beginning. She went above and beyond the call of duty this time, going through the manuscript not once, not twice, but three times before she felt I'd 'nailed it.' I am so thankful for her!

I'm also grateful for the Christian Indie Authors Facebook group and my sister bloggers at Inspy Romance. These folks make a difference in my life every single day. I'm thrilled to walk beside them as we tell stories for Jesus!

Thank you to my Facebook friends, followers, street team, and reader group members for prayers, encouragement, and great fellowship. If you'd like to join other readers who love my stories, please find us at Valerie Comer: Readers Group.

Thanks to my husband, Jim, whose love for me never fails and who encourages me in every endeavor. Thanks to my kids, their spouses, and my wonderful grandgirls for cheering me on. To them, having an author for a mom/grandma is "normal." Imagine that!

All my love and gratitude goes to Jesus, the One who is my vision, the High King of Heaven, the lord of my heart. Thank you. A thousand times, thank you.

ABOUT VALERIE COMER

Valerie Comer's life on a small farm in western Canada provides the seed for stories of contemporary Christian romance. Like many of her characters, Valerie grows much of her own food and is active in the local foods movement as well as her church. She only hopes her imaginary friends enjoy their happily-ever-afters as much as she does hers, shared with her husband, adult kids, and adorable grand-daughters.

Valerie is a *USA Today* bestselling author and a two-time Word Award winner. She writes engaging characters, strong communities, and deep faith into her green clean romances.

To find out more, visit her website at www.valeriecomer.com, where you can read her blog, explore her many links, and sign up for her email newsletter, where you will find news, giveaways, deals, book recommendations and more. You can also find Valerie blogging with other authors of Christian contemporary romance at Inspy Romance.